THE LIBERATION OF SITA

Praise for *The Liberation of Sita*

Volga retells the story of Sita for thoughtful women today. Steeped in epic, mythic, and ecological discourse, *The Liberation of Sita* illuminates Sita's inner thoughts, revealing how she values flowers, sculpture, meditation, and eventually attains inner peace. This eminently engaging book also contains an extensive interview with the author and an insightful introduction. – Professor Paula Richman, editor of *Modern Ramayana Stories in South India*.

Volga's voice – strong, clear and fearless – pierces through these translations and reminds us that women have always read the Ramayana differently from men, finding our own friends, our own truths and our own inspirations in the story. – Arshia Sattar

THE LIBERATION OF SITA

VOLGA

Translated from the Telugu by

T. Vijay Kumar
C. Vijayasree

HARPERPERENNIAL

HARPERPERENNIAL

First published in India in 2016 by Harper Perennial
An imprint of HarperCollins *Publishers*
4th Floor, Tower A, Building No. 10, DLF Cyber City,
DLF Phase II, Gurugram, Haryana – 122002
www.harpercollins.co.in

This edition published in India in 2018 by Harper Perennial

22

P-ISBN: 978-93-5277-501-9
E-ISBN: 978-93-5277-502-6

Typeset in 11/16 Charter BT
by Jojy Philip, New Delhi

Printed and bound at
Thomson Press (India) Ltd

FSC www.fsc.org MIX Paper | Supporting responsible forestry FSC® C010615

This book is produced from independently certified FSC® paper to ensure responsible forest management.

HarperCollins *Publishers*, Macken House, 39/40 Mayor Street Upper,
Dublin 1, D01 C9W8, Ireland

Dedicated to the memory of

Dr C. Vijayasree

(1953–2012)

Dedicated to the memory of

Contents

The Reunion

Sunset time. The forest, with crimson brightness on one side and engulfing darkness on the other, was like a red furnace emitting black smoke. Birds flying in rows were returning to their nests, filling the forest with their clamour. Herds of deer were getting ready for a moonlight excursion, shedding their daytime lethargy. The sage's ashram in that thick forest looked beautiful—and tranquil—like the creation of an accomplished painter.

In the ashram the evening rituals had begun. Sacrificial fires were glowing. Mantras were being chanted in solemn tones. The women of the hermitage, having watered the plants, were relaxing. Some of them were weaving garlands for the puja. Children, having returned from their forest wanderings, nestled in the embrace of their mothers, who had been eagerly waiting for them. Some mothers were hurrying their children along for the evening ablutions. In one small cottage, a mother was waiting for her children who had not yet come back from the forest. From the look in her eyes, it was clear that she lived only for the children. There was anxiety in those kind, fear-filled eyes.

Her name was Sita.

She was waiting for her two sons.

They would normally return by this time every day, bringing some wild flowers with them. They would plead with their mother to use these nameless flowers for worship, and Sita would refuse. So they would give the flowers some strange names. When their mother laughed at their ingenuity, they would sulk. Sita would then appease them by using the flowers for the puja. As darkness thickened, the two boys would sing in full-throated ease and the forest listened to them with rapture.

Lava and Kusa had not yet returned. Sita did not apprehend any danger; the boys knew the forest like the back of their hands. They were born there; they had grown up there; they were the sons of the forest. But what was the reason for the delay? Ever since their visit to Ayodhya, Sita's heart was filled with an anxiety that she never had felt before. A strange disturbance plagued her mind—fear not of the forest, but of the city. As the sky darkened, Sita's eyes began to glow like lamps.

Just then the two boys walked into that light. Sita heaved a sigh of relief and asked them why they were late. Lava said, 'Look, Mother,' and emptied the flowers he had brought in his angavastram into a plate.

Flowers—red, white, yellow—filled the plate with wild smiles. Such flowers had never been seen before. The fragrance too was hitherto unknown. Kusa and Lava looked at their mother, proud of their find.

'Where did you get these from? So pretty!' said Sita, touching the petals tenderly.

'Mother, we discovered a new garden today. We have never seen such a garden before. Even the divine garden Valmiki taata told us about is no match for it,' Kusa said.

Lava nodded, endorsing his brother's words.

'Whose garden is that, Kusa?' Sita asked.

'Mother, the garden is so beautiful but its owner is so ugly. She came out when we were plucking the flowers. We got scared. Anna gathered courage somehow and told her, "We are from the ashram. We are collecting flowers for worship." Then we hurried out.' His face contorted with disgust.

'Her form was so hideous! She was so ugly,' Lava recalled with a shudder.

'That's wrong, son. Never loathe people for their looks. She has grown a very nice garden even though she is ugly, hasn't she?' said Sita.

'The rest of her is all right, Mother. But she didn't have a nose or ears. Instead, there were big holes in her face, as if someone had carved them out.'

Sita flinched as if someone had whipped her. 'No ears or nose?'

'Maybe she had them before. It looked like someone had chopped them off. Isn't that so, brother?'

Sita was sure now. It must be Surpanakha! Yes, it is definitely Surpanakha.

Eighteen years ago ... Surpanakha came seeking Rama's love. What a pretty woman! The wicked prank played by Rama and Lakshmana left her horribly disfigured. Poor thing! Is Surpanakha living in this forest now? So much time has passed since then!

Since Rama insulted Surpanakha, Ravana wanted to take revenge on Rama by abducting me.

Do women exist only to be used by men to settle their scores? Rama and Lakshmana would not have done this to Surpanakha if they did not know that she was Ravana's sister. Rama's objective was to provoke Ravana; his mission, to find a cause to start a quarrel with Ravana, was accomplished through Surpanakha.

It was all politics.

Poor Surpanakha came longing for love. Who will love that ugly woman now that she has lost her ears and nose?

Has she spent all her life in lovelessness?

Has she showered all her love on that garden?

Has she created the garden as an expression of her passion for beauty?

Are these flowers a manifestation of the tenderness of her heart?

Poor Surpanakha!

Lava and Kusa were surprised to see the tears in their mother's eyes.

'What is this, Mother? Why are you getting so distressed hearing about some stranger's ugliness?'

Sita wiped her tears and said with a smile, 'Will you take me to that garden tomorrow?'

Lava and Kusa looked at each other in disbelief.

'Really, I would like to go with you. Will you take me there? Do you remember the way?'

The brothers' joy soared to the skies at Sita's words.

They were filled with excitement at the thought of their mother accompanying them on an excursion into the forest. They had always wanted to show her all the places in the forest that they were familiar with. But Sita never went out with them. On the few occasions she did go outdoors, it was always with the other women of the hermitage. Walking through the impenetrable jungle holding their mother's hands, giving her courage so she would not get scared, showing her all the marvels of the place—the very thought filled the boys with irrepressible joy.

They were impatient for dawn to break.

The night passed pensively for Sita, too. Memories of the past confronted her, however hard she tried to push them aside.

Surpanakha's coming—how beautifully she had walked in. White jasmines in her hair. Garlands of yellow ganneru around her neck. Bracelets of nilambara on her wrists. She was like a walking creeper in bloom.

She looked curiously at my jewellery as if wondering why I burdened myself with all that metal, which had neither fragrance nor grace. She only looked at me, didn't say a word. She went up straight to Rama. I kept doing my work, while paying attention to their conversation. After a while, there was bloodshed in the ashram.

A woman's heart-rending cry!

How much must she have cursed us for that act!

That curse has still not left us it seems.

No man will ever love her.

The man who loved me abandoned me.

Have the two stories become one and the same, finally?

What will Surpanakha say when she sees me?

She may not speak to me out of anger—yet I must see her. I must see Surpanakha.

The next morning, Lava and Kusa set out with Sita after she had completed her chores.

'Mother, I'll show you my Raja today,' said Lava.

An elephant in musth, roaming freely in the forest, had been tamed by Lava. The two brothers wandered around the forest riding the elephant.

'Mother, won't you sit on the elephant?' asked Lava, fondly.

'No, son, I prefer walking,' said Sita, remembering the days when she would go in a procession, sitting atop the royal elephant.

The brothers thought Sita was afraid of riding the elephant.

'Poor Mother! How can she climb onto the elephant? She is scared,' Kusa chided Lava.

The two brothers led their mother towards the garden, introducing all the creatures they had befriended along the way.

Absorbed in her children's chatter, Sita did not feel the strain of the journey at all.

'Mother, this is the garden.'

Sita stood dumbfounded. The garden looked like the very smile of nature. Even Ashoka Vanam would pale in comparison.

You are blessed, Surpanakha! she thought.

'Come, Mother, let's go in,' said the children.

'I'll go in by myself. You go around the forest and come back here in the evening. We'll go back to the ashram together,' Sita told them.

She saw a woman at some distance. Though her face was turned away, Sita could tell it was Surpanakha.

She went closer and called out gently, 'Surpanakha!'

Surpanakha turned around. She did not recognize Sita.

'Who are you, amma? Have you lost your way? How do you know my name?' she asked.

'I have not lost my way, Surpanakha. I have come looking for the right path. I'm Sita.'

Surpanakha was stunned.

Sita? Is she Sita? How much she has changed!

Surpanakha only knew the Sita covered in jewellery. Moreover, she had never taken a close look at her.

Is this Sita, the consort of Chakravarthi Sri Ramachandra, who slayed Ravana and extended the Aryan Empire across the entire south?

Surpanakha could not believe it.

Why this coarse sari? Why these garlands for jewellery? Why this sun-singed golden complexion?

Is she Sita? Sri Rama's wife, Sita?

'Sita—you mean, Sri Ramachandra's ...'

Stopping Surpanakha before she could complete the question, Sita said with quiet dignity, 'I am Sita. I am Janaka's daughter, Janaki. I am the daughter of Mother Earth.'

'What about Sri Rama?' Surpanakha was confused.

'Sri Rama has abandoned me. I'm now living in Valmiki's ashram.'

Surpanakha had no words to speak. Sri Rama abandoned Sita! Surpanakha knew about the love between Sita and Rama better than anyone else. And the price she had paid for it, too, was not small.

Was anguish inevitable for women who love Sri Rama?

On Sita's face, Surpanakha could only see peace and dignity; there was no trace of distress.

Sita has matured a lot, thought Surpanakha.

'Yesterday, my children saw your garden. They saw you too. Today, they brought me here. Your garden is so beautiful and peaceful,' said Sita with a smile.

'Were those your boys? How charming they were!' Surpanakha said.

A fleeting expression of pride crossed Sita's face. It did not miss Surpanakha's attention.

'All the creepers, plants and trees in this garden are my children,' Surpanakha said.

'Yes, that's why they're so beautiful!' agreed Sita.

Pride stood firm in Surpanakha's eyes.

'Tell me, Surpanakha, how has your life been?'

'As beautiful and joyous as this garden.'

'I am happy to hear that, Surpanakha. I was worried about you after the humiliation you suffered. I knew how you hankered after beauty; I was worried that, unable to accept your own mutilation, you might have resorted to something extreme. I was troubled by such thoughts whenever I remembered you.'

Surpanakha was moved by the kindness and affection in Sita's eyes.

A feeling of friendship sprouted in their hearts and thrilled them.

'You're a brave woman,' Sita said.

Sita's sincere words of appreciation overwhelmed Surpanakha. She felt a strong desire to narrate the course of her life to Sita.

'Don't look at how I am today and imagine that all this happened easily, Sita. I have become tough by facing upto the challenges life threw at me. I have been able to find happiness in trying to understand the very meaning of beauty.

'My life was unbearable in the initial days after the mutilation.

'I loathed my own appearance. I hated myself. There were also days when I even wanted to kill myself.

'I want beauty. I want love. I can't live without them. But I, who was such a worshipper of beauty, was turned into an ugly figure.

'Looking at my ugliness, men—all the handsome men that I desired—used to abhor me.

'Those days were hellish. I saw no point in living. My heart burned with pain and anger every single day. How much I cursed Sri Rama, his brother Lakshmana and you! I spewed venom at all of you. There was not a trace of love left in me; hate had gripped my heart. I, who loved beauty, began hating everything that was beautiful. My love of beauty turned into jealousy of all those who were beautiful.

'I became a walking volcano. A stormy sea of grief.'

Their hearts grew heavy with the recollection of Surpanakha's painful memories.

'How did you come out of such sorrow, Surpanakha?'

'It was hard. It was hard finding the real meaning of beauty. I was so proud of my beauty. You don't know how much I adored my nose. The sharp noses of you, Aryans, looked strange to me. There's beauty in strangeness, too, of course. My nose was neither sharp nor flat. It was, I thought, exactly how Eshwar must have conceived the perfect nose in the beginning of Creation. I was so proud of my nose! I used to adorn it with yellow and white wild flowers which shone like stars on either side. When my lovers tenderly kissed the tip of my nose, it used to arouse me.

'No one except I will understand what it meant to lose such a nose. I endured all that misery. I endured the burden of all those perverted thoughts that arose out of my disfigurement. Sometimes I felt like disfiguring everyone, everything.

'To come out of that spitefulness, to love beauty once again, to understand the essence of form and formlessness—I had to wage a huge battle against myself. My only collaborator in that battle was this infinite nature.

'I struggled a lot to grasp that there is no difference between beauty and ugliness in nature. I observed many living creatures and understood that movement and stillness are one and the same. I discovered the secrets of colours. I had no guru in this matter. I pursued it on my own. I searched every particle in nature, and in the course of that search, my own vision has changed. Everything began to look beautiful to my eyes. I, who hated everything including myself, began to love everything including myself.

'To recognize that the response evoked in me by a little bird, which had been pecked and displumed by its fellow birds, was a feeling at once of love and beauty, and to seize that response and understand its meaning—the effort I made to achieve all this was extraordinary.

'Gradually I learned to love my hands. I learned how to create, work and serve with those hands. It took more than ten years for all this to happen. After ten years of rigorous practice and hard work bore fruit, I began growing this garden.'

Surpanakha unravelled before Sita the beauty and truth of her life's journey.

'How beautiful you are, Surpanakha! How does it matter whether any man appreciates your beauty or not,' Sita's voice choked.

Surpanakha's trial was no less than the trial by fire

that I had to go through—Sita thought and it brought tears to her eyes.

But Surpanakha laughed, beautifully, joyously.

'Why? Don't men have eyes? Don't they have a heart? I'm not talking about men who only know how to disfigure and to hate the disfigured.'

'You mean ...' Sita did not complete the sentence but its meaning was clear.

'Your guess is correct, Sita. I found the companionship of a man. There is a man who could own for a while the beauty that flows into nature through my hands and could surrender himself to me.' So saying Surpanakha called out, 'Sudhira!'

A strong, well-built man, who perfectly fit the description of his name, appeared.

'This is Sita.'

Sudhira greeted Sita respectfully, with folded hands.

'I just called you to introduce you to Sita.'

At this, Sudhira turned back and left. In that moment's interaction, Sita could see that there was between them a relationship which she had not seen before between any man and woman.

'You've made your life a success, haven't you?' Sita asked.

'I've realized that the meaning of success for a woman does not lie in her relationship with a man. Only after that realization, did I find this man's companionship.'

Sita intently listened to Surpanakha's words. There

was a rare wisdom and dignity in her words. One felt like listening to her again and again.

'Sita—what about you?'

'I find fulfillment in bringing up my sons.'

'Is that the goal of your life?'

'Yes. I'm Rama's wife. As the queen, I couldn't discharge my duties. I must at least give to Ramarajya its heirs.'

'You never lived in that kingdom, yet see how your life is entangled in it, Sita!'

'Yes, being a king's wife, it is inevitable, isn't it?' Sita smiled.

'I don't know why, but I was always afraid of kingdoms. Despite my brother's persuasion, I never lived in the city of Lanka. The joy you get from wandering in a forest, you don't get anywhere else.'

'I too like the forest life. When Rama abandoned me, this forest softened my suffering.'

Time simply flew as they conversed.

'My children do not know that they are Sri Rama's sons. I have not told them. They'll know when the time comes.'

'Once they get to know, you think they'll live even for a minute more in the forest?' Surpanakha looked pityingly at Sita.

'They too love this forest life' Sita said feebly.

'They may like it. But the kingdom has no love for the forest. For the development of cities and for the protection of the citizens, it may become inevitable for children of the forest to migrate.'

Sita too knew it was inevitable.

'What will you do then? Will you stay back alone at Valmiki's ashram?'

'No, Surpanakha. I will take refuge in my mother, Bhudevi.'

'Isn't your mother omnipresent, Sita? I think your mother is manifest more beautifully here than anywhere else.'

Surpanakha proudly surveyed her garden.

Sita smiled, having understood Surpanakha's suggestion. Her heart swelled with joy at Surpanakha's unsolicited affection. She felt a bond of sisterhood with her.

'I will certainly come, Surpanakha. After my children leave me and go to the city, I will become the daughter of Mother Earth. Resting under these cool trees, I shall create a new meaning for my life.'

Their conversation stopped as the children returned.

Surpanakha gave the children ripe fruits from her garden, which they ate with relish.

'Mother, who is she?' they enquired on their way back.

'She is someone very close to me. A dear friend.'

'But you never told us about her.'

'You'll know everything at the right time. But never

forget the way to this garden in this forest. Wherever you may go, whatever you may do, never forget this path.'

'We will not forget, Mother,' Lava and Kusa promised.

Music of the Earth

Janaka's palace, aglow with music, dance, the fragrance of flowers and ineffable joy and excitement, looked like an illuminated boat floating on the waves of joy.

Naturally! Janaka's dearest daughter Sita had been given in marriage to the handsome Sri Ramachandra, who broke the bow of Parasurama. Alongside, Sita's sisters were married to Rama's brothers. Ayodhya and Videha came together, and the capital rejoiced in that embrace.

Midnight. The din of celebrations had subsided. There was no sound except that of the footsteps of the maids who stayed awake to attend to the needs of the royal household. In those silent first nights, the young couples were in raptures, looking into each other's eyes.

In just two nights, Sita Devi became close enough to Sri Rama to be able to converse with him freely and playfully. Rama too grew out of his innocence about what he should do with Sita's beauty.

Though well past midnight, neither of them had any thought of going to bed. Casual conversation, banter, jokes, witty exchanges, needless laughter, silly tantrums and elaborate appeasements! That spacious room was abounding with the excitement of love.

Rama was telling her, with a little exaggeration, about the many demons he had slain, and how effortlessly, while accompanying Viswamitra. But Sita did not want to hear about killings in that hour. She gently stopped Rama.

'During your journey into the forest, other than this devastation, did nothing wonderful happen, Rama?' asked Sita, tousling the black locks of his hair.

'As it is I'm dark. If you pull my hair over my face like that, I won't even be visible,' Rama said, pushing Sita's hand aside.

'Your asking reminds me that I saw an amazing beauty during my journey, Sita!' he said.

Sita's face fell. How could Rama see some other beauty before he set eyes on me?

Rama noticed Sita's face lose its lustre. He did not have the age or the heart yet to tease Sita with the description of the beauty of another woman. So he told Sita everything.

'When I saw her, I felt like greeting her with folded hands. She was the wife of a sage. Ahalya, I am told, is her name. When I looked at her large eyes, I felt frightened for a moment, finding in them the depth of an ocean that contains both fire and ice. Her enigmatic smile still haunts me. Anger, grace, detachment, compassion, love—everything was there in that smile. The symmetry of her body was not just physical; it was a balance that comes from gaining control over both mind and body through rigorous discipline. I felt like staring at her forever. Involuntarily, I raised my hands and greeted her with reverence. She smiled graciously like a goddess. Sage Viswamitra interrupted then and, leading me away, told me her story. My heart turned bitter. I was sad to know that there was no character behind that beauty. Yet I could not forget her. I can't forget those eyes and that smile.'

Sita was listening eagerly.

Ahalya. A beautiful name that means 'land untouched by a plough'. I am the daughter of Earth tilled with a plough. The one who does not even know the stroke of a plough is Ahalya. What does Rama mean by lack of character? Can I ask him?

Rama noticed that Sita was lost in thought. He drew her closer and said, 'When I'm with you, your thoughts can't be elsewhere. If your mind veers away from me even for a fleeting moment, I can't bear it.'

Although he spoke affectionately, there was a firm authority in his voice that unsettled Sita. So she blurted out her thoughts quickly.

'My mind did not wander elsewhere. I am thinking about what you said about Ahalya. What does lack of character ...'

'Sita, you're still very young. You won't understand. You shouldn't even hear such things or talk about them.'

Rama sealed her lips with his. Sita forgot everything in the intoxication of that kiss.

Sita had no leisure even to reflect upon how time simply went by in Ayodhya. Rama's love left her breathless. The indulgence of her mothers-in-law was boundless. There was no scope for her to miss her parental home. Her sisters were with her anyway. Other than complimenting her playmates for adorning her with different flowers everyday, she had nothing much to do.

One day during those blissful times, Kausalya asked for Sita to be brought to her chambers. After dressing up appropriately, Sita offered her salutations to her mother-in-law.

The wives of some feudatories had come to call on Sita. When they saw her, they were awed by her beauty and their open admiration delighted Kausalya.

'Our Sita is the daughter of Mother Earth,' announced Kausalya with pride.

'Yes, we have heard. It's Maharaja Janaka's good fortune. That's why she has surpassed Ahalya in beauty,' said one of the queens.

Sita started. Ahalya—the one whom Rama had admired—is she known to these women, too?

The guests left. Kausalya called the maids and got them to ward off the evil eye cast on Sita.

'I can neither stop myself from showing you off nor stop worrying about the effect of the evil eye on you,' smiled Kausalya.

'Who is Ahalya, Mother-in-law?' Sita asked hesitantly.

'The wife of Maharshi Gautama, child. An exceptional beauty with a noble character befitting her beauty. Unfortunately she was accursed.'

'What happened, Mother-in-law?'

'What is there to tell, child. As you know, men consider women objects of enjoyment. Someone named Indra lusted after her. One day, when Gautama was not in the ashram, Indra arrived disguised as Gautama. Ahalya mistook him for her husband and satiated his desire. When Gautama returned, the truth came out. The Maharshi disowned her. When she realized what had happened, Ahalya was stupefied. Turned almost into a lifeless rock. Now she lives in the forest, outside our world, without a shelter, and indifferent to the sun, rain or cold. Refuses to see anyone.'

Noticing the tears in Sita's eyes, Kausalya stopped, full of regret for what she had said.

'You are still a child. I made a mistake by telling you all these things. Whatever is written in one's fate will happen. There is nothing we can do. No one can change one's fate. Forget it, my child. Forget about that ill-fated woman.' To divert her mind, Kausalya led Sita out of her chambers and towards the cage of the talking parrot.

As soon as the parrot saw them, it turned towards Sita and prattled in a strange sing-song: 'Sita-fate', 'Sita-destiny'.

Sita was scared and, hiding behind Kausalya, asked, 'Can I go back to my chambers, Mother-in-law?'

Kausalya too was flustered by the parrot's strange behaviour. 'Let's go, child. I'll come with you and see Rama.' Stopping the maids from accompanying her, Kausalya walked towards the couple's chambers. Sita had been waiting for Rama since the afternoon. Hearing that Rama had still not returned, Kausalya stayed with Sita till the evening. When it was time for the evening puja, she left after inviting Sita and Rama to her chambers the next morning.

Sita's mind was full of disquiet. Recalling the story of Ahalya, she felt frightened, sorry, sad. She also felt angry because she could not understand why Rama called her characterless. Didn't Mother-in-law say she was a woman of noble character? When she was not at fault for what had happened, why did Rama call her that? Poor Ahalya! Mother-in-law said it was her fate. Why did the parrot chirp like that? 'Sita-fate', 'Sita-destiny'? She trembled at the memory of those words. Sita had developed a splitting headache by now, and drifted into sleep with it.

The antahpuram or women's quarters in the palace was drowned in an ocean of sorrow. Overcoming it, Sita, Rama and Lakshmana reached the banks of the river. After bidding farewell to the close confidants who accompanied them, they stepped into a boat. It was only then that Sita felt relieved. She started thinking ...

Whatever has happened has happened. How does it matter where I am as long as I am with Rama? Antahpurams have been familiar to me since childhood. Let me experience the peace and comfort of these rivers, forests and mountains. Rama's love will be entirely mine without the interruption of politics.

Sita's natural temperament was to take pleasure in what she had. When they crossed the boundaries of their kingdom, the only feeling she had was of returning home. She never felt as if she was travelling to an alien land. When she mentioned this to Rama, he said with a smile, 'You are the daughter of Earth, aren't you? So, all this is your empire.' Sita remembered Ahalya once again. She did not know why, whenever someone called her the daughter of Earth, she thought of Ahalya.

The journey continued. Whenever they came across an ashram in the forest, Rama halted and met the sages and listened to their problems. As they narrated the problems created by the aboriginals, Rama's grip on his bow tightened. Meanwhile, Sita met the wives of the sages and learned the recipes of various dishes from them.

On the whole, time passed quite pleasantly for Sita. The two brothers, Rama and Lakshmana, decided to stay at a sage's ashram for a couple of days. They were trying to gather information about the aboriginals in the neighbourhood. After completing the morning puja, the brothers went out. When Sita tried to assist the sage's wife, she dissuaded her. So, coming to know of a waterfall in the vicinity, Sita asked for directions and set out for it.

It wasn't very far. It wasn't even a big waterfall. But it was beautiful. Small streams of clear water flowed from the waterfall. At the bottom of the stream, pebbles of different hues sparkled like a string of jewels when the sun's rays hit them. Sita sat with her feet in the water, observing the coloured stones.

Sita was lost in the world of those multicoloured stones till she heard a soft, deep voice asking her, 'Who are you, my dear?'

When Sita turned around and looked up, she was stunned by the sight of the woman beside her. A figure of dazzling brightness! Instinctively, Sita got up and greeted her with folded hands.

'My name is Sita. The wife of Sri Ramachandra.'

She placed her hand on Sita's shoulder and said with a smile, 'I see.'

That there could be so much kindness in a smile, Sita had not known until then.

'Who are you, Mother?' Sita asked, looking at her feet.

'I'm called Ahalya.'

Sita's heart skipped a beat.

'Ahalya! You are Ahalya?'

'Have you heard about me?' Ahalya laughed. Her laughter sounded like a cascade of parijata flowers.

As Ahalya sat down, Sita sat next to her.

'Yes, I have heard. My mother-in-law, Kausalya, told me the entire story. How unjust!'

'What is so unjust?' Ahalya asked matter-of-factly.

'You were accused of a crime you did not commit,' Sita said with sympathy.

'Aren't many women in this world wrongly accused, Sita?'

'But wasn't it outrageous in your case? After all, you did not know that he was not your husband ...'

'Do you know whether I knew this or not? Does anyone know?'

Sita began to say something but stopped herself. She felt dazed. Recovering, she asked hesitantly, 'You mean ... you knew?'

'That question has no meaning, Sita.'

'But then, what is the truth? If there is something called truth, wouldn't it have a meaning?'

Sita was surprised and full of curiosity.

'Each one to their own truth. Does anyone in this world have the power to decide between truth and untruth?'

Looking at the mix of confusion and innocence on Sita's face, Ahalya took pity on her.

'I know it is difficult to understand, Sita. I don't know why my story was told to you and how it was narrated. Indra lusted after me. Like everyone else, he too looked at women as if they are meant for men's enjoyment. Knowing that I wouldn't surrender to his desire, he came in the hours of darkness in the guise of my husband. Did I see through his disguise? That is the question that bothers many people in this world. But to my husband, the question was irrelevant. It was the same to him either way. His property, even if temporarily, had fallen into the hands of another. It was polluted. Pollution, cleanliness, purity, impurity, honour, dishonour—Brahmin men have invested these words with such power that there is no scope in them for truth and untruth. No distinction.'

Ahalya stopped. Did Sita understand any of this? Looking at her, she felt a strange affection. She was surprised at her own willingness to share her story with Sita. Why did she feel this bond of sisterhood with her?

'Why did you come to this forest, Sita?'

Sita narrated her entire story.

'You could not stay without Rama and so you came after him to dwell in the forest,' smiled Ahalya.

She felt agitated, anguished. She wanted the comfort of Rama's presence immediately. She got up and folded her hands in farewell.

Ahalya placed her hand on Sita's head and, blessing her, said, 'Never agree to a trial, Sita. Don't bow down to authority.'

As if she could not bear to listen to those words, Sita left in a hurry and walked away without looking back.

That night after telling Rama about her day, Sita said softly, 'I met Ahalya.'

'Where?' Rama jumped up.

'Why are you so alarmed? I went near the waterfall.'

'Alone?'

'Yes. It's close by and very serene.'

'Don't go anywhere alone, Sita,' Rama said, sounding worried.

'All right, I won't. Will you not allow me to tell you about Ahalya?'

Rama did not say anything.

'As you said, she is a rare beauty. You feel like folding your hands in reverence at her splendour. But what she said made no sense. That there is no such thing called truth, that the truth keeps changing—she said all kinds of things. They didn't sound pleasant to me. I felt annoyed.'

Rama listened to her in silence.

'Why don't you say something?'

'What is there to say? Innocent people like you with

pure hearts will never understand what women like her say. Go to sleep, Sita, it's quite late.'

He said it almost like an order and went to sleep himself.

Sita wanted to recount to Rama the entire conversation, but she understood that he was not interested in the details.

Ahalya's words kept coming back to her, and annoyed and disturbed, she spent a sleepless night.

After that, for a long time, she more or less forgot about Ahalya.

That day, Sita's heart was filled with joyous excitement. She heard the news of Ravana's slaying. She rejoiced at the thought of release from Lanka. Her heart was aflutter in anticipation of meeting Rama. How would she react on seeing Rama? What would Rama say? His affection, love, touch ... She was going to have it all again. Tears of joy flowed freely from her eyes. Seeing Lakshmana in the distance, Sita walked quickly towards him.

The look on Lakshmana's face surprised her. Hadn't Ravana been slain? Then why wasn't there joy on Lakshmana's face? Instead of walking with his head held high in the pride of victory, why was he walking with his head bowed, like a culprit?

'How are you, Lakshmana?' Sita enquired. Lakshmana bowed his head further.

'Sri Ramachandra, your brother, is he well?' Sita had no misgivings about Rama's well-being. But looking at the gloomy face of her brother-in-law, she couldn't think of anything else to ask.

'He is well, Sister-in-law.'

'Then why do you look so sad, Lakshmana? Why isn't your face cheerful? Your brother has sent you to fetch me, hasn't he? Let us go then.'

'I should tell you something, Sister-in-law.'

Sita was beginning to panic. On the one hand, the din made by the victorious vanara sena could be heard even in Ashoka Vanam. Then why did Lakshmana look like someone completely defeated?

'Sri Ramachandra wants you to undergo a chastity test, Sister-in-law.'

When the words sank into her heart, Sita could barely stand. She collapsed to the ground.

'Sri Ramachandra has no misgivings whatsoever, Sister-in-law. It's only for the sake of the people. Justice alone will prevail in the trial. Truth will triumph. Everyone will applaud your character once you withstand the test. Sri Ramachandra has asked me to convey this to you, Sister-in-law.'

The image of Ahalya flashed across Sita's mind.

What does conducting an enquiry mean, Sita? Distrust, isn't it? Wouldn't it be better, instead, to believe in either your innocence or guilt? … All men are the same, Sita.

Did Ahalya know it would turn out like this? Rama

has asked for my chastity test. Isn't death better than this? Isn't leaving me to my fate better? Why humiliate me like this? Why wage such a war if this is how I was going to be treated?

War is for demonstrating the valour of men. Rama has proved his heroism. He is awaiting the demonstration of his wife's chastity. Isn't this what Ahalya called distrust?

Wouldn't accepting her in trust or rejecting her in distrust be better? What should be done now? Sita's heart was like a volcano.

'Don't misunderstand Sri Rama, Sister-in-law. This is just a measure to keep anyone from saying anything unpleasant about you later. You should walk into Ayodhya like a glowing fire. You can't imagine how distressed and distraught my brother is. But he really is helpless, Sister-in-law.'

As Lakshmana described Rama's despondency, the burning in Sita's heart subsided.

Rama has no misgivings. He knows the truth. He is doing this for my sake, to save me from any accusation. He must be agonizing over my response. He must be tormented by the thought of the gulf this could create between us.

Sita prepared herself to console Rama.

He is helpless. A weakling. But against whom? Not against Ravana but against society. Against its moral principles, its code of justice. Sita recalled Ahalya's words once again:

Pollution, cleanliness, purity, impurity, honour, dishonour—Brahmin men have invested these words with such power that …

Rama's arrow will fail against that power. Brahma's weapon will wane. Rama has to be rescued. He has to be protected from this society. His tears have to be wiped. He has to be given strength. No one but she can do it.

No, Ahalya, Rama has no distrust. My Rama is not like other men. This is the truth. I may not be able to prove it to you. The world may not believe it. But for me that is the truth.

Didn't Ahalya say that too …

Each one to their own truth. Does anyone in this world have the power to decide between truth and untruth?

Ahalya, why did you utter these words? I am beginning to grasp their meaning now. But is my understanding correct? Who can tell me?

Sita held her head with both hands as if it were going to split.

Leave all these thoughts for later. First I should see Rama. I should face the trial boldly.

Sita stood up and wiped her face clean with her sari's end.

'Let's go, Lakshmana. Let's go to your brother. Let me see what this test is.'

Lakshmana looked up in surprise at these bold words of resolve.

Sita is the daughter of Earth, he thought he heard a whisper in his ears.

Even after coming back to Ayodhya, Sita was unable to forget Ahalya. She felt diffident even as she set foot in the antahpuram. Would she be able to bear it if any one of her three mothers-in-law mentioned the trial?

When Kausalya embraced her and said with tears running down her face, 'My daughter-in-law is a chaste woman,' Sita felt a hardness, a steeliness enter her soul. Why is Mother-in-law so relieved at the confirmation of my chastity? Did she doubt me? That was how she had thought of Ahalya too.

Ahalya had said, *'Whatever gives you peace of mind, that alone is the truth, Sita.'* Did Mother-in-law too think similarly or did she trust me?

These were questions with no answers. There was no one Sita could confer with, and no one talked openly about what had happened. Rama was behaving as if nothing had transpired. There was no change in his love. He showed the same affection. What would Ahalya think of her? Would she laugh at her? *'Never agree to a trial, Sita,'* she had said. But Sita agreed to it. Would Ahalya believe her if she said that she had agreed to it not for herself but for the sake of Rama? Would she be able to understand Sita's decision? Ahalya was a gnani.

She would definitely understand. Sita's desire to meet Ahalya grew stronger by the day.

She would not be able to talk to anybody else the way she could with Ahalya. And if Sita did not confide in someone soon, her heart would harden even more.

Even when the entire antahpuram was celebrating the news of Sita's pregnancy, Sita spent the day thinking about Ahalya.

'It seems pregnant women have a lot of cravings that have to be satisfied. Mother insists that I find out your heart's desires, Sita,' said Rama to her one day.

Although Sita felt like telling Rama that her heart's desire was to meet Ahalya and to talk to her, she restrained herself. Rama would be hurt. He wouldn't like it. But then again, if her wish remained unfulfilled, it would not do any good to her mind or to the foetus in her womb.

'I feel like going on an outing in the forest, Rama. I wish to once again visit those ashrams, river banks, and enjoy the beauty of the wilderness.'

'That's not a difficult wish to fulfil. We shall certainly go.'

Sita felt excited and apprehensive at the same time. Why did she initiate this venture? If she spoke to Ahalya, the unrest in her mind would only increase, not decrease. Was she simply inviting trouble? No. She had gained enough experience to not be annoyed by Ahalya's words. Unless she listened to Ahalya's wise words, she would not attain peace. Ahalya alone had the power to calm her agitated mind.

Although she would be accompanying Rama, Sita was determined to find an opportunity to meet Ahalya by herself.

Gradually Sita's heart filled with happiness. Her face lit up with the eagerness of one who was going to meet her dearest friend. Looking at her cheerful face, Rama too rejoiced. He thought, everything will settle down after the visit to the forest. It would have been wonderful if Sita had returned to Ayodhya from the forest and not from Lanka. But that wasn't to be. Now an opportunity had come up again. After they returned from the forest, Sita would present him with an heir. With that, everything would change. The thin veil of awkwardness that had come between Sita and him would be lifted.

That night, Rama slept as peacefully as he used to during their forest sojourn.

When she came to know that Rama was not accompanying her on the visit to the forest, Sita relaxed. Now she could spend as much time with Ahalya as she wanted. She could empty her heart out to her without any restraint.

Boarding the chariot happily, Sita was surprised by the gloomy look on Lakshmana's face.

'Are you not well, Lakshmana? Why didn't you assign this task to Shatrugna?'

Without a reply, Lakshmana took the reins into his hands and stirred the horses. Sita gave him the landmarks near the waterfall that she wanted to visit. But Lakshmana stopped the chariot well before the destination, before the woods turned thick.

On Valmiki's instructions, the inmates of the ashram were looking after a pregnant Sita with extreme care.

Sita looked like a frozen River Ganga. Seeing her thus, Valmiki wondered, how do we prepare her for easy labour?

He said to Sita, 'If you want something, tell me without any hesitation, my child.'

'I wish to meet Ahalya,' Sita said, looking straight into Valmiki's eyes.

Valmiki was taken aback for a moment. Recovering, he said, 'As you wish, Sita. She is certainly capable of giving you solace. I'll send her a message.'

After Sita had waited for her for two days without any other thought on her mind, Ahalya arrived in Valmiki's ashram.

'How are you, Sita?' Ahalya asked affectionately, sitting next to her and taking her hands in hers. Sita buried her face in Ahalya's lap and sobbed inconsolably.

'Don't cry, my child. Such grief is not good for you in your condition.' Even as she consoled Sita, there was a thin film of tears in Ahalya's eyes. After crying her heart out, Sita said, 'Now my heart feels lighter, sister. Since the time of Ravana's slaying, my heart has gradually been hardening. After seeing you, and after receiving your affectionate touch, my heart is tender once again.'

They talked to each other in silence for a long time.

'Now I understand the meaning of what you said about truth and untruth, sister.'

'There is no better path to wisdom than experience, my child.'

'I agreed to the trial only for the sake of Rama, not for my own.'

'Don't I know that.'

'But again … will my decision haunt me forever?'

'Till you take decisions for Rama's sake and not yours, it will continue to pursue you, Sita. Look at yourself. You are enduring great pain. You think you are enduring it for the sake of someone else. You think that you have performed your duty for the sake of someone else. Your courage, your self-confidence … you have surrendered everything to others. What have you saved for yourself?'

'What is "I", sister? Who am I?'

Ahalya smiled.

'The greatest of sages and philosophers have spent their lifetimes in search of an answer to this question. You means you, nothing else. You are not just the wife of Rama. There is something more in you, something that is your own. No one counsels women to find out what that something more is. If men's pride is in wealth, or valour, or education, or caste–sect, for women it lies in fidelity, motherhood. No one advises women to transcend that pride. Most often, women don't realize that they are part of the wider world. They limit themselves to an individual, to a household, to a family's honour. Conquering the ego becomes the goal of spirituality for men. For women, to nourish that ego and to burn themselves to ashes in it becomes the goal. Sita, try to understand who you are, what the goal of your life is. It is not easy at all. But don't give up. You will discover the truth in the end. You have that ability. You have saved Sri Ramachandra, can't you save yourself? Don't grieve over what has already happened. It is all for your own good, and is part of the process of self-realization. Be happy. Observe nature and the evolution of life. Notice the continual changes in them. The forest doesn't comprise ashrams alone. There are also people of many races in it. Observe their lives. You belong to this whole world, not just to Rama.'

Ahalya's words sounded like the music of the earth. Sita was listening to her attentively.

'You are about to experience motherhood. Enjoy that too. Bring up your children without nurturing any hopes and expectations; be like the doe that rears fawns.'

Sita's latent maternal instinct welled up. As if on their own, her hands caressed her swollen belly. Her eyes sparkled with the glow of love and life.

The next morning, Ahalya got ready to leave.

Noticing the lustre in Sita's eyes, Valmiki was relieved.

Sita embraced Ahalya.

'Sita, shall I tell you what the truth is in my case?'

'Don't, sister. It's all the same. It has no meaning.'

Sita gave her a respectful send-off.

Holding the boys to his breast, Rama became ecstatic.

Having accepted his sons as Ayodhya's heirs, wouldn't the state accept Sita as its queen? After that, he would not care about what anyone said.

He sent a message asking Sita to return to Ayodhya.

When she received the message, Sita remained equanimous. The glow of contentment that had brightened her face in the last twelve years did not diminish even a bit.

She declined Rama's request with a smile.

'Can you live without your children, Sita?' Another message arrived at the ashram from Ayodhya.

Rama thought that Sita would succumb to this appeal to her sentiments.

'These children are not just my children, Rama. They are symbols of the life force of this universe. I have realized that they belong to the whole universe. Of course, you, and they too, believe that they belong to Ayodhya and are the heirs of Raghu Vamsa. You should act according to your belief.'

'Then what about you, Sita … without a husband, children?'

'I am the daughter of Earth, Rama. I have realized who I am. The whole universe belongs to me. I don't lack anything. I am the daughter of Earth.'

Rama was left speechless by those solemn words.

Devoid of Sita's support, Rama tasted defeat for the first time in his life. By refusing to bow down to external authority, Sita had fully experienced, for the first time, the inner power of self-authority.

The Sand Pot

The forest in spring. So many hues, so many fragrances! An intoxicating fragrance from the mango trees scattered here and there. Melodious songs of the kokilas! Sita was witnessing the glory of spring for the first time and enjoying it to her heart's content. On one of those days, she noticed the women of a neighbouring ashram go out in a group. She was curious to know where they were all going. But before she could call out to them, they had gone out of earshot. When she asked Lakshmana, he said he did not know where the women were going. They could find out when they returned in the evening, he said. But no one knew when they came back. Those who had gone out in a group returned individually, perhaps.

Next morning, after completing her chores, and after Rama and Lakshmana bid her farewell to go into the forest, Sita went to Shanta's ashram, which was nearby.

As soon as she entered the ashram, she was pleasantly surprised. There were two beautiful statues, and five or six pots with attractive pictures on them, arranged in a beautiful pattern. Sita looked at them in delight and asked, 'Where did you get these from, Shanta? They were not there when I visited you the other day.'

'We had all gone to Renuka Devi's shrine of sculptures. I picked up what I liked,' said Shanta.

'Renuka Devi?' asked Sita, curiously.

'You don't know her, Sita. You're new to this place. Renuka Devi's shrine of sculptures is about a half-hour walk from here. Every year we all go there, and get the pots, stone vessels and statues we want. We went there yesterday. We should have asked you to join us,' said Shanta.

'There is such skill in Renuka Devi's hands?' asked Sita, surprised.

'Of course! Not just these. She has many more, which are even better. She knows all the secrets of the art of sculpture. Once she starts work, it's like she's meditating. There are few sages who are so absorbed, even in meditation. While you look at these artefacts, Sita, I'll go fetch a couple of pots of water.' Shanta went out of the ashram.

Renuka Devi—that name evoked some old memories in Sita's mind.

She was familiar with the name—when—where? Then Sita remembered her swayamvaram. She also remembered the commotion that followed soon after Rama had broken Shiva's bow and she had turned to go back into the antahpuram after adorning Rama's neck with a garland.

Who was he? He had rushed in like a volcanic mountain and burst upon Rama like an apocalyptic cloud.

The women of the antahpuram had taken Sita inside. Sita struggled hard to recall their conversations of that day.

'Parasurama is a great warrior. He is the one who vowed that he would not let kshatriyas live on Earth—What will happen now? What will this Brahmin do to Rama?' Sita had trembled at her companion's words.

'Not only a valiant warrior, but a hard-souled man. He is so cruel that he did not even hesitate to cut off his mother's head,' another woman wailed. Sita had trembled even more with fear. Noticing this, everyone stopped talking and started comforting her. She was shedding tears, anxious for Rama. The ecstasy she had experienced on seeing Rama, the pride she had felt at his valour, the feeling that she experienced in such a short span of time that Rama was her everything—she was afraid that all these would be taken away. Not that she did not have confidence in Rama's courage, but Parasurama's ruthlessness brought tears to her eyes. He had killed his own mother! Sita's head reeled.

Just then two of her companions came running. 'Parasurama has calmed down; he has approved of Rama's valour. They have struck up a friendship and reached an agreement.'

Hearing this, it was as if life returned to Sita. Later, her father came and consoled her. He told her that whatever had happened was for the best as it proved Rama's valour beyond doubt. He blessed her, saying that she was fortunate to get a heroic man like Rama as her husband.

A few months later, after the bustle of the wedding celebrations subsided, Sita broached the subject of Parasurama with Rama while recalling the events of the wedding. Rama at once started praising Parasurama.

'How is it that you are praising a person who has slain kshatriyas?' Sita asked.

'The kshatriyas he killed were those who did not observe Arya Dharma. He has firmly established Arya Dharma in the entire northern plain. When he got to know that I revere Arya Dharma, he was pleased. He accepted me as his heir and handed me the responsibility of spreading the dharma in the entire southern plain.'

'How will you …'

Before Sita could complete her sentence. Rama said, 'What is to happen will happen—why these questions?'

'But he almost killed his mother, I heard.'

'That was on his father's order. What could he have

done? Is there a higher dharma than carrying out the wishes of one's father?'

Before they could complete their conversation, Rama received a summons from Dasaratha. When Rama returned, he gave Sita the happy news of his coronation. The palace was filled with joy on the occasion. But the next day everything turned upside down. As their banishment to the forest was announced, the coronation remained a dream.

After so many years, the name of Renuka Devi brought back memories of Parasurama. Is this the same Renuka Devi whom Parasurama had nearly killed?

Sita found the answer soon, when she met Renuka Devi accidentally.

When Sita went to bathe in the river, she saw some women filling their pots with mud and sand. Among them she saw a woman who stood out, and was instantly enamoured.

Though old, Renuka was strong. Grey hair. Determination in her large eyes. Peaceful countenance. A smile of contentment on her lips. Sita looked at her without blinking.

The woman too got into the river with Sita. As they were bathing, she said, 'I have not seen you before. Who are you? Are you new to this place?'

Sita introduced herself.

'Are you the wife of Rama, who has set out to spread Arya Dharma in the forests as well?' asked Renuka, sounding a little scornful.

'He has come to the forest obeying his father's injunction,' Sita said firmly, ignoring the scorn.

'That too is part of Arya Dharma, I know. To blindly carry out a father's wish without thinking about justice or injustice. My son did the same thing. Your husband promised my son that he too would perform the same task and establish Arya Dharma among the other races in the country.' There was dignity in Renuka's voice.

'Are you Renuka Devi?' asked Sita, though she was in no doubt.

'Yes. You may have heard about me. Come to my ashram with me,' Renuka Devi said. It was almost an order.

'Forgive me. I cannot come,' Sita replied politely.

Renuka laughed. To Sita, her laughter sounded like a river in its exuberance.

'Why? Will your husband object?'

'No, no. I've never talked to him about you.'

'Then why hesitate? Let's go.'

Sita found the liberty Renuka was taking with her—like a mother—a little strange.

She remained silent.

'Come to my ashram with me. You will like the sculptures and paintings there.'

'I'll come some other time, after taking permission from Sri Ramachandra.'

'Your husband will not give you permission.' Renuka laughed again.

'How do you know?' Sita asked sharply.

'No one knows as much as I do about husbands and sons.' Renuka's laughter floated up like foam.

'Your husband and son may have done you an injustice. But it is not fair to conclude that everyone is like that. I'll come to your ashram some other time.'

Sita bid farewell to Renuka with folded hands and turned around, leaving no scope for further conversation.

Renuka Devi's face remained engraved in Sita's memory. The familiarity in her words, the authority in her laughter kept coming back to her mind. 'She invited me like a mother would. What if I visit her once—what will happen if I visit Renuka Devi's ashram after Rama and Lakshmana leave for the forest one day?' she wondered.

The desire to visit Renuka Devi's shrine of sculptures and to talk to her grew stronger in Sita.

She told Rama.

'There is a shrine of sculptures close by, I've heard. A few days ago, the wives of all the hermits went there and brought back some sculptures and pots. They're so beautiful I too would like to go there and bring some.'

'Yes, I have heard about that shrine. But why do you want to go? Let Lakshmana go and get them. Can you carry those heavy things?'

'I'll see them all and select what I like. We'll see about bringing them here later.'

'All right. Go and select what you like,' said Rama. Does Rama know about Renuka Devi? Since he has heard about the shrine of sculptures, perhaps he does. He may have respect for Parasurama's mother. Rama may not know that she is resentful of his and Parasurama's dharma. What do I know for that matter?

Convinced that unless she met Renuka Devi her questions would remain unanswered, Sita rushed through her chores so she could go to the shrinc of sculptures.

Following Shanta's directions, Sita reached Renuka Devi's ashram quite easily. Renuka was engrossed in her work. A few other women were working alongside her with mud and sand. Seeing Sita, Renuka stood up, setting her work aside.

'Have you come here with your husband's permission?' she asked with a smile.

'Yes, I have come with his permission. What is wrong with that? What is so strange about it? Will you show me the sculptures, please?' said Sita.

Renuka took her inside, smiling affectionately. Sita was dumbfounded to see the wealth of sculptures there. The art of sculpture was not unknown to Sita, who grew up in the royal palaces of Mithila and Ayodhya. But these sculptures—they were different, Sita had never seen this style of sculpting. It was unique, thought Sita, and said so.

'These have been made by female sculptors. My students and I sculpted them. They are different, and abstract.' Renuka took Sita to another part of the shrine.

'See, here you have sculptures that are made in the more conventional style.'

They too were beautiful. And their beauty owed little to outward form. There was in them a conspicuous dignity, strength and composure.

Sita selected some.

'Generally women do not get into the art of sculpting. How did you learn this? Who did you learn it from?'

'I had an interest in it since childhood. I have no teachers—I'm my own teacher.' Renuka smiled and brought Sita something to eat.

'See, I'm giving this to you specially. This is a pot made of sand—a sand pot.' She handed it to Sita.

'A pot made of sand?'

'Yes, I alone have this skill.'

'It's wonderful.'

'Yes, it is a wonder. Every woman must have one of these,' Renuka said with a smile.

'Why?'

'If they understand that their paativratyam and fidelity are like these sand pots, they will be able to live in peace.'

Sita was confused.

'To make this pot, you need a lot of concentration. Those who did not know this thought I was making a miracle happen by virtue of my chastity, my paativratyam. Since there was no flaw in my character anyway, I let them think what they liked. Concentration can be broken at any time. The cause may be anything. In my case, a man became the cause of distraction. My husband was enraged. He believed that my paativratyam was violated by the mere act of looking at that man. A good pot is a product of many things—practice, concentration, sand, the right amount of water and so on. Sage Jamadagni was a man of great wisdom, yet he did not understand such a simple truth. But such is the wisdom of these spiritual seekers. No matter how much wisdom they earn through penance, they continue to have a dogmatic view on the paativratyam of their wives.'

Sarcasm was evident in Renuka's voice.

'What happened then?' asked Sita anxiously.

'He ordered our sons to kill me. Parasurama came forward to do it. He began chopping my head. When my head was half-cut, my husband's fury abated. He asked Parasurama to stop. Women in the ashram and the tribal women who live in the forest healed me and made my head stand on my neck again. For months, I vacillated between life and death. In front of me—I, who had returned from the threshold of death—were three figures: of my husband, whom I had served with my thoughts, words and deeds, and my wifehood; of my son, whom I had carried for ten months, given birth to and raised, and my motherhood; and of this pot, the result of my focus and my art. All three are the same. They are shattered by the slightest cause and life hangs on a sword's edge.'

Tears filled Sita's eyes. Renuka retained her composure.

'Lot of questions came up during that struggle between life and death. Are such bonds, with a husband and sons, necessary for women? I thought they were not, so I moved away from them. I am living with my art. I give the same advice to my students. I don't make a sand pot often. I make it occasionally so that I don't forget the fragile nature of paativratyam.'

'Does a woman have a world other than her husband's? Is there a higher meaning to a woman's life than motherhood? Your experience may have been different. But to preach everyone on the basis of your experience …'

'A woman thinks she doesn't have a world other than that of her husband's. True. But some day that very husband will tell her that there is no place for her in his world. Then what's left for her? She thinks giving birth to sons is the ultimate goal of her life. But those sons become heirs to their father, and even before we realize it, they leave her hands and go under the wing of their father. They submit to his authority. Or they begin to legislate our lives. Why bear such sons? Nobody will experience this as harshly as I have. Having realized this bitter truth, isn't it my responsibility to share it with other women? But you Brahmins give no value for my words anyway. I teach my skills to people of different tribes in this forest and give them the essence of my experience.'

'But won't creation come to an end if there is no bond of marriage?'

'Why would it come to an end, Sita? Many creatures take birth and grow in this forest. They have no marital bonds, do they? There are people of different tribes whose customs are different from yours.'

'Does that mean human beings should live like animals, uncivilized?'

'Why do you look down upon animals, Sita? We should love animals and nature. We should worship them. We should befriend them. That's the duty of humans. Ignoring that basic duty, you think what is written in books is civilization. Is that right? You have come to the forest from the city. Why insist so much on the civilization of the cities? Isn't nature the best teacher?'

'I don't understand your words. I feel they will cause harm to women.'

'They certainly won't. When a child belongs to its mother, there is no harm in that. A situation where children ask their mother who their father is or where a husband asks his wife who fathered her children comes only in the lives of some women, Sita. Think of the predicament of those women, and you'll understand my words.'

'Just because something happened to someone,

somewhere, should people remain without marrying and bear children outside wedlock? Does it happen anywhere? Is that good conduct?' asked Sita resentfully.

'I don't know if it is good conduct or not—I speak of what I know. It is only through experience that one understands the truth. And whatever you understand, you tell others.'

'Your truth and mine are not the same.'

'Perhaps not. As you see more of the world, you may understand the truth of my words, too.'

It seemed like a futile discussion to Sita. As she got up in a huff, her right foot knocked over the sand pot near her feet. The pot broke.

Sita was terrified. There was anxiety on Renuka's face too. She drew Sita close and embraced her.

'You have great strength, Sita. Don't forget my words. May your strength be your protection, I bless you.'

Sita touched Renuka's feet involuntarily and left.

Renuka sat down where she was, a vague concern about Sita troubling her mind.

Sita was busy raising her two sons. She did not know how eight years had gone by in Valmiki's ashram. After formally initiating her children into education and sending them to Valmiki for schooling, she managed to get some spare time. Even then her thoughts centred around her sons. Until they returned home, no matter what work she was engaged in, her eyes would remain riveted on the door. Their sweet words, their melodious voices singing the saga of Rama, their pranks. Sita's life was passing quite happily. One day, Kusa and Lava walked in silently, without looking at their mother standing on the threshold. Each went to a corner and sat down with a glum face. Surprised, Sita came in and, amused by their sulking faces, asked, 'What happened, children? Why do you look so glum?'

'Amma, who is our father?'

'Amma, are we kshatriyas?'

Sita's face turned pale. She had no intention of telling them that they were Sri Rama's sons.

She felt a constriction in her chest. Her heart convulsed.

A situation where children ask their mother who their father is or where a husband asks his wife who fathered her children comes only in the lives of some women, Sita. Think of the predicament of those women and you'll understand my words. As Renuka's words rang in her ears, blood rushed to her face and from there into her head. It took Sita some time to come out of that turmoil and get a hold on herself. Slowly she regained her composure. These questions were bound to come—if not today, some other day. She must answer them. Some innocent children in the ashram must have asked Kusa and Lava these questions and the boys must have been been confused, anguished even. She must give her sons the strength to answer all such questions. Sita embraced her children.

'You are, indeed, kshatriya boys,' she said, kissing them.

'Our father?' Both of them asked in one voice.

'Your father is a great hero by the name Saketha. He is engaged in a great mission for the welfare of mankind. It's such a huge mission that he doesn't have a moment's respite. Since it is not possible for him to think of anything other than his mission, he left us at this ashram of Valmiki.'

'What is that mission, Amma?' Kusa's innocent face brimmed with respect for the unknown mission.

'It is a noble effort to help everyone in this world lead a life free from suffering. I do not know the details.'

'After accomplishing his mission, will Father come for us, Amma?'

'He'll surely come. He'll embrace you and take you with him.'

The two boys, happiness blooming on their faces, laughed merrily.

'Now go and fetch flowers for my puja,' said Sita. Lava and Kusa did not feel like stirring. For the first time, they had learnt something about their father. He was a kshatriya. A great man on a great mission for the welfare of mankind. But Lava had a question.

'Amma, is our father a warrior? A kshatriya must be good at archery and warfare. Is our father skilled in those?'

Sita smiled with pride.

'There is no one on Earth who can match your father in those skills.'

The two boys embraced their mother.

'Amma, we do not know when our father will accomplish his mission and return. How do we learn a kshatriya's skills? Who, in this ashram, can teach us those skills? What will our father think of us when he comes back, Amma? What shall we do?'

Sita could not suppress her smile, seeing their anxiety.

'You want to master kshatriya skills. Is that all? I'll teach you.'

'You?'

'Of course. I'm a kshatriya woman, am I not?'

'But women don't fight wars, do they?'

'When necessary, they'll do anything. I'm adept at all those skills. From tomorrow, I'm not only your mother but also your teacher.' The children jumped for joy.

Sita took Valmiki's permission and started teaching Lava and Kusa archery. The boys were surprised to see their mother's expertise.

They always loved their mother; now, they also felt proud of her. With the sole aim of becoming great warriors by the time their father returned, the boys started learning new skills from her. When not training with her, they relaxed by singing the saga of Rama to Valmiki. As Sita watched her children grow, she began to worry more and more. They were bringing up the subject of their father everyday on some pretext or the other. Seeing their eagerness to meet their father, Sita's heart grew heavy.

'Amma, when will our father return?' Lava asked, pitifully.

Sita held her children close to her.

'You have to be patient for some more time, my sons. As I told you, he has been living incognito for some reason. At present, no one should know his real identity. At the right time, you will get to know everything.'

'It would be wonderful if that time came soon, wouldn't it, mother?' Kusa's face shone with wistfulness.

'Yes, it would be. But what is it that you lack even now? Taatayya is giving you lessons and I'm teaching you archery. There is a lot more that I need to teach you.'

'When what you have to teach us is completed, will Father come and teach us the rest?'

Sita laughed.

'When I've taught you all that I can, there'll be nothing left for your father to teach.'

'Does that mean you know more than Father does?'

'It's not about more or less, son. There used to be a great bow at one time. There were very few who could lift it and shoot an arrow with it. Your father and I were equally adept at that.'

'Amma, please teach us that skill. If we master it by the time Father comes and demonstrate it to him, he will be surprised, won't he?'

'I have a lot of work to do. I can't sit here chatting with you.' Sita got up and went to the back of the ashram. She had no work really. She did not want to work either.

The children were pining for their father. They were dreaming about him. Though she had brought them up like they were her very life, though they knew nothing about their father, though their father did not even know about their birth or growing up—they wanted him. Sons needed to grow up inheriting their father's name.

She was Janaki—daughter of Mother Earth. Yet, she became Janaki—daughter of Janaka—under his care. These boys would get recognition only when they were regarded as Rama's offspring. Rama was Dasarathi—'of Dasaratha'—he was fond of that name, revered it and took pride in it. These children too wanted that kind of acknowledgement. It was indeed the order of the world.

But would that happen? Would Rama embrace these children? Would he give them his name? Would he acknowledge them as descendants of his family? If that did not happen, how these innocent hearts would grieve!

If Rama accepted them as his children and took them to Ayodhya, what would happen to her?

She had left her father who loved her like his own life and taken Rama's hand.

Rama, whom she loved like her own life, had let go of her hand.

These children whom she had brought up, caring for

them like her own life—would she be able to hold on to them? Should she even attempt to do that? Would they remain in her grasp even if she did? Would they not run to their father if he called them?

What did she have, other than the disgrace that Rama, bowing to public opinion, had heaped on her?

In comparison, Rama had a kingdom—which was so dear to him that he could not give it up even for her sake. Would these children give up such a kingdom for her sake? Would their kshatriya blood allow them to do that?

Sita's mind was in turmoil.

As a mother she had no power over them. Power never fascinated her anyway. She only had love—she loved her father; she loved Rama; she loved her children. There was no desire for power in any of those relationships. She did not want it.

These children were nature's gift to her. She had raised them like fawns. When fawns grow up, they go off into the forest, never to return.

These children too …

Sita struggled to rein in her mind.

It had been ten days since Lava and Kusa left for Ayodhya with Valmiki. For those ten days, Sita had no control over her mind.

Would the children be able to meet Sri Ramachandra

in Ayodhya? Would he recognize them? Would he ask Valmiki about them? When Valmiki unravelled the truth, how would he respond? How would the children respond—when they got to know that Rama was their father? When they found out that their mother was none other than Sita, the wife of Sri Ramachandra, their joy would know no bounds. But after that? When everything became clear, if Rama came to take his children, would they leave her and go with him? Would Rama ask her to come too?

Even if he did, would she go?

What if the children refused to go without her?

But they wouldn't. They had respect for their father, they were proud of him.

After what she had told them about their father, they considered him no less than a god.

She had gaven birth to them, brought them up to surpass their father in heroism. But she had to let them go. When their father claimed them, she could not hold them back, saying they were hers. They belonged to Raghu Vamsa. They must continue the dynasty.

Again, Sita remembered Renuka.

Renuka's words had caused aversion in Sita that day. Now she could understand Renuka's pain. The day Rama demanded a trial by fire, the day he sent her away into the forest, Sita remembered the sand pot Renuka had made. Ahalya, Renuka, Sita—they were all victims of mistrust and humiliation.

When Sita felt wretched after Rama abandoned her, it was Ahalya who had nursed her back to normalcy.

That day Ahalya must have cautioned her through foresight.

She had told Sita to bring her children up like a pair of fawns without any attachment. Sita had no great ambitions for her sons. But the thought of separation from her children wrenched her heart. The moans of the umbilical bond sometimes rang through her entire body. A blanket of emptiness descends on her mind. If the moon's glow in front of your eyes vanishes suddenly, what is left? Only pitch darkness.

Who would hold her hand and guide her through that darkness?

'Am I not here, my girl?' The affectionate words of Mother Earth gave her the strength of a thousand elephants.

Her mother was independent. She would go to her mother. Her mother was omnipotent. So she could take Sita into her embrace. Sita had now seen it all—sons, fathers, sons' obedience to fathers, wives' faithfulness to husbands, motherhood. But there was one thing she had not seen. Nor had Ahalya, Surpanakha or Urmila experienced it. It was what Renuka had faced—the brutality of her own son. She had seen the dharma-bound cruelty of her son who, taking his father's word as the word of the Vedas, was ready to hack her head off. She then realized what the foundation of that cruelty was. How many whirlpools must have stirred in her heart then? And how deep they must have been? In fact, so deep as to challenge Arya Dharma itself.

Did she have Renuka's strength? After returning the heirs to the family, she would return to her mother's lap, detached. That was all. But even that was defiance of Arya Dharma, wasn't it?

Surpanakha, Ahalya, Renuka, Urmila—each one had a story of her own. Each one had followed a path of her own. Her path, her way, was hers alone.

Sita had learnt what she could from their experiences. At first, she felt only disdain and anger for them. Later, when she understood that the anguish in their lives was similar, she felt a camaraderie, a companionship with them. When Sita heard the sufferings of others, she realized that she was not alone. The awareness that she was one of them gave her strength. And it was that strength which enabled her to withstand the disgrace and bear her children, to give them a happy childhood and to train them in all the skills.

Valmiki came in just then, breaking Sita's train of thought. She respectfully spread a mat for him.

'Amma, Rama grasped everything. He recognized Lava and Kusa as his children. He was ready to accept them honourably.'

Valmiki's voice was filled with happiness. He had discharged his duty. Sri Rama's children, the children of the hero of his epic, having been well trained in his ashram, would soon be joining their father. He was excited and he exulted that his epic was going to end on a happy note with the union of Sri Rama and his sons.

Sita said calmly, 'That's good, isn't it, O Sage,' and kept quiet. Suddenly his enthusiasm waned.

What about Sita? Valmiki thought.

'Amma, Rama has asked you to affirm the truth in the royal court, in the presence of the courtiers. After that you'll be the queen. Mother of heroes, queen mother.'

Sita felt like laughing out loud. She controlled herself, out of respect for Valmiki, and said with a smile, 'Do I need to do that? Is there any sense in such an effort?'

Valmiki was dumbstruck. But he understood Sita's mind, which was strong and steady.

'I have neither the power nor the courage to advise you, daughter!' He put his hand on her head, blessed her silently and left.

Sita busied herself with preparations for her journey. She had to leave before Lava and Kusa returned. There were many from whom she must take leave.

Lava and Kusa returned and were dejected to find the ashram empty. They now knew the whole story about their mother.

They charged up to Valmiki, to ask about her.

Valmiki told them what Sita had said.

For the first time, they were angry with their mother.

How nice it would have been had she come to the court once and proved her innocence as their father desired! It would have been so good for them. A thin flame burned in their young hearts.

They were not little boys growing up in an ashram any more. They were Aryan heirs, princes, future kings. Sita, on the other hand, was the daughter of Mother Earth. Would she ever be understood?

The Liberated

When Sita, Rama and Lakshmana returned to Ayodhya after fourteen years of vanvaas, and crossing an ocean of hardships, the entire royal household turned up to welcome them.

Except Urmila.

Sita's eyes searched eagerly for Urmila, but in vain. The embrace of her mothers-in-law, enquiries about their well-being, the friendly words of Mandavi and Srutakirthi—none of these warmed Sita's heart.

After the initial excitement abated, Sita drew her sister Srutakirthi close and asked gently, 'Where is Urmila? Is she not well?'

Srutakirthi's face turned pale. This scared Sita.

'What happened to Urmila? She is well, isn't she?'

Though Srutakirthi understood Sita's anxiety, she did not know what to say.

It had been fourteen years since Srutakirthi last saw Urmila.

'Why do you stare like that without answering? Where is Urmila? How is she?' Sita asked again.

'I don't know how Urmila is. I have not seen her since you left.'

Sita thought she had misheard Srutakirthi. So she asked again, this time louder, 'Srutakirthi, I'm asking about Urmila.'

'I'm telling you about Urmila. No one has seen her since you left. She never came out of her palace. She allowed no one to enter her palace either.'

Sita was shocked.

'No one, not even our mothers-in-law?'

'No one. Only the servants keep going in and out, and only one of them—Charumati—is allowed to enter her room. She keeps us informed of Urmila's well-being.'

Sita felt choked.

Fourteen years—how did she live without talking to anyone and without meeting her own people? How deeply she must have been hurt to have taken such a decision! Fourteen years! Will she forgive me, Rama and Lakshmana?

'Does Urmila know that we were to arrive today?'

Srutakirthi looked down.

Sita wanted to see Rama at once, but he was surrounded by his brothers, ministers and other prominent people from the city. It was almost impossible to approach him or Lakshmana.

Just then, Srutakirthi brought a woman to Sita and said, 'This is Charumati.' Sita did not wait any longer.

'Come, let's go to Urmila.'

'She will not see anyone,' Charumati said curtly.

'When she learns that those very people who are responsible for her life in isolation have come to see her, she will definitely meet them. Let's go.'

With a stern look, Sita ordered Charumati to move. It appeared as though Urmila's palace was hundreds of miles away. Why was it taking so long to get there ...

During their life in the forest, Sita always felt that it would have been wonderful if Urmila too had been with them, along with Lakshmana. When Rama and Lakshmana are away attending to their work in the forest, Urmila and I could have enjoyed the fragrances of the forest! she used to think.

Why didn't Lakshmana bring Urmila? Whenever she broached the subject, Lakshmana kept quiet.

When they had set out for life in the forest, everything was in a state of confusion.

Dasaratha's illness, Kausalya's sorrow, the entire royal household was in utter disorder. To persuade everyone to let her accompany Rama was in itself a huge task. It was only when calm set in, and when they were crossing the River Sarayu, that it struck Sita that Urmila was not with them. She recalled that Urmila had no role to play in the entire episode and that she had not even come out to bid them farewell.

She asked Rama over and over again.

'Didn't Urmila want to come? She must have cried a lot to see Lakshmana go. Did she think forest life would be too tough? Then Lakshmana too should have stayed back in Ayodhya. Is it fair to leave her alone in the palace for our sake?'

Rama used to pacify her with some explanation or the other: Urmila had to stay in Ayodhya to serve the mothers-in-law. Who would look after Kausalya? Sita could have provided support to her widowed mother-in-law, who was separated from her son. But she had come to live in the forest. So who else was there now for Kausalya except Urmila? Shouldn't there be at least three daughters-in-law for the three mothers-in-law? But, more importantly, someone had to take care of Mother Kausalya.

Rama would give many such reasons.

Being a part of the royal household involved carrying out several responsibilities. As the queen, Kausalya used to manage them with great efficiency. Now she did not have the strength for that, nor was she interested any longer. Who could bear the burden of that responsibility but Urmila?

'Tell me, Sita! Isn't Urmila more capable than you in such matters? When we were in Ayodhya, Mother used to entrust more responsibilities to Urmila than to you, didn't she?'

'Yes.' Sita would slip into contemplation. Urmila was very capable in these matters. She could rule with a mere glance. She knew all about the duties of a royal household. Father, too, used to praise her on that count.

'The interest you show in archery and in the outdoors—you don't in other matters, Sita!' Father used to say.

True. Sita never liked the authority wielded by the royal household or its administration. Playing in the garden, practising archery, relaxing amidst nature—these were enough for Sita. After going to Ayodhya, she showed no interest in taking over the household responsibilities from her mother-in-law. But Urmila was always with Kausalya.

Sita felt happier in the forest than in Ayodhya. Here she had people she could make friends with rather than lord over. She loved this companionship.

'There's no rule that Urmila should like the same things that you do. You are the daughter of Earth. A lover of nature. Urmila may prefer city life and the responsibilities of a royal household …' No matter how much Rama tried to convince her, Sita would remain worried about Urmila.

To be separated from one's husband—isn't that the most miserable ordeal to suffer?

Sita understood how miserable it was while in Ravana's captivity.

Knowing Sita's love for nature, Ravana confined her in Ashoka Vanam. The beauty of that garden was indescribable. She had not seen anything like it in Mithila or Ayodhya. Ravana bragged a lot but never had the courage to even stare at Sita. And Sita treated him like a blade of grass.

Yet, Sita was reduced to waiting for her husband to come to her rescue—and this was unbearable for her.

Rama will come, he will kill Ravana—Sita had no doubt about this. But restraining her own powers of self-protection, sitting and waiting without doing anything—Sita found it an ordeal.

But she knew Rama's mind well. He was determined that Ravana's death should be at his hands. She had to withhold her own powers to let Rama fulfil his duty.

'In our relationship, what is it that you like the most?' Sita had asked Rama one day.

'Protecting you like an eyelid protects the eye. If a thorn pierces your foot, I must pluck it out. I must, myself, kill the wild animals that approach you. The thought that I'm protecting you gives me greater pride and pleasure than sovereignty over Ayodhya,' Rama had said.

'I can protect myself. I can match you in archery,' Sita had said, laughing. Rama's face had fallen.

'As long as I am alive, you will never have to protect yourself. Such a situation must never arise. You must look towards me for protection. You must turn to my strong arms for protection. If you take care of yourself, what am I for? Promise me that you will never do that.'

Sita had placed her hand in Rama's.

Abduction. Waiting in Ashoka Vanam—Sita had no alternative. In those moments of separation from her husband, Sita often thought of Urmila.

How is Urmila bearing this sorrow? My dear sister, why did you stay back in Ayodhya? Why were you so attached to the royal household?—Sita would include Urmila in her suffering.

Finally Ravana was killed. The test of fire followed.

'Ayodhya is awaiting the arrival of Sita and Rama.' Even when Rama announced this proudly, Sita was actually yearning to see Urmila.

'How happy Urmila must be, how beautifully she must have decorated her palace, how she would have adorned herself to appear before Lakshmana! As soon as we reach the royal household, after paying my respects to my mothers-in-law, I must go to Urmila along with Lakshmana. Never mind if it delays their much awaited reunion by a few minutes … I must first visit Urmila before I go to my palace.' Sita would rejoice in imagining this scene.

'How beautiful your joyous face looks, Sita!' said Rama.

'Just the thought of Urmila's happiness is making me happy,' Sita said, smiling sweetly.

Rama shared Sita's joy. Both of them looked at Lakshmana meaningfully and smiled.

Rama's heart swelled with pride as he looked at his brother who, for his sake, had endured fourteen years of separation from his wife.

He drew Lakshmana close and hugged him.

Lakshmana was thrilled by the affection in his brother's embrace. As they approached the city, the hearts of all three were like the sea at high tide on a full moon night.

So many thoughts, so many memories ... But when Sita arrived, filled with excitement, Urmila was not present to welcome her or to be embraced.

Then came the heart-rending news of Urmila's self-imposed exile of fourteen years.

Urmila's palace was all decorated on the outside. But the doors of her room remained shut. Charumati knocked gently on the door and said, 'Amma! Your sister, Janaki Devi, has come to see you.'

Sita was nervous.

How will Urmila look? What will she say? What will she ask me? How should I respond? The doors did not open.

Sita called out herself.

'Urmila, it's me, your sister. I'll tell you everything. Please forgive us and open the door.'

The doors of Urmila's room opened.

Urmila stood in front of her. Sita was shocked for a moment. This was not the Urmila she knew. There was innocence in those eyes earlier. Some royal haughtiness too. Her stately mien was that of a queen. What was it that glowed in those eyes? There was a rare poise and dignity in the way she carried herself. What was that radiance in her face? While Sita was still recovering, Urmila came closer, touched her feet and sat her down.

'Urmila, I've been thinking about you these fourteen years. I'm very sorry.' Tears welled up in Sita's eyes.

'You must be angry with us.'

Urmila smiled lovingly but solemnly.

'I'm not angry with anyone.'

'Then why did you distance yourself like this? If you were not angry, why did you lock yourself up in a room like this? Express your anger, your wrath. But do not isolate yourself. Tell me what happened; why are you doing this?'

Urmila smiled.

'I'll tell you, Akka—who else can I speak to? No one else will understand. That's why I've been silent.'

Sita waited eagerly.

'Akka, initially I did close these doors in anger. My husband left me without uttering a word to me, without any concern for my opinion, without even giving me a thought, devoting himself entirely to his brother. That day I burned in fury. I wanted to turn this royal household upside down with my revolt.

'Everyone was grieving for you all. No one even looked at me. In helpless anger, I too decided not to look at anyone. I began my protest.'

Sita was trying to understand Urmila.

'When I began, it was, indeed, wrath. But gradually it turned into a quest for truth—within me and with myself. Why so much fury—fury that consumed me—fury that wanted to burn everyone? Why this anguish? I knew the cause. But a longing to delve deeper into that cause was born in me without my noticing it. What is anger? What is sorrow? What is joy? What is the relation between my body and these feelings and emotions that I experience? Many such questions—they engulfed me. I began to observe my body, my thoughts, and the emotions they triggered within me. Any distraction to this process annoyed me. That's why I desired solitude. Not loneliness, solitude. The solitude in which I could converse within and with myself.

'That conversation brought me and the people related to me face to face. It dissected relationships. I began to probe the essence of each of my relationships—with Father, with you, Lakshmana, Sri Rama, Kausalya—peeling them layer by layer.

'I loved you as my elder sister. But when you went away with your husband, abandoning me, something changed in our relationship. What was that change? What was its nature? Why did it happen?

'Jealousy, hatred, love, respect—what's the real

difference between these feelings? Is there any difference at all or are they merely shades of the same feeling? How does light barge into shadow, and shadow encroach on light? Which is light and which is shadow?

'As one question after another rose within me, I experienced something akin to the thrill of a battle. I heard that our husbands fought many battles during these fourteen years to slay demons. I don't know whether those battles resulted in peace or not. But the war I waged with these questions has brought me peace and joy.'

That peace was evident on Urmila's face. Sita looked at her in amazement, listening to her words and imagining the battle Urmila had fought. She began to worry about Lakshmana.

'Lakshmana loves you, Urmila! With him—'

Urmila interrupted Sita.

'We are going to see each other after fourteen years. I have changed a lot. Change is the sign of life. The course of our future depends on the value he attaches to that change.

'I've acquired the wisdom to ask questions not out of hatred but for the sake of justice. My relationship with Lakshmana will depend on whether he understands my wisdom and how much he respects it.

'Will he give up his authority over me even while being bound to and enjoying his other powers? I don't know, and can't say. Whatever happens, my peace will not be disturbed. The question is, does he want that peace or not?'

Even as she spoke, Urmila saw and understood the anxiety on Sita's face.

Will her anxiety abate if I explain things further? Urmila wanted to try.

'When I understood my relationships with others, I felt I understood everything. Power is the root cause of all sorrow, Akka. Do you know another strange thing? We must acquire this power. And then give it up. I shall not submit to anyone's power. Nor will I bind anyone with my power. Then I will feel I have liberated myself. I will feel only joy within myself! Great peace! Much love! Compassion for all!

'It's a pity how people get bogged down by structures of power. Unable to see how they can liberate themselves, they rot in unrest, sorrow and hatred.

'I wonder if I should share this secret to achieving peace with everyone.

'But who will understand?

'Will those who consider my fourteen-year-long meditation in search of truth mere sleep understand my words?

'They concluded that I was sleeping. Do they know the difference between sleep and wakefulness?

'Did they ever sleep peacefully? Were they ever truly awake and conscious?

'They say I was asleep—they will label me as mad if they hear what I have to say.'

'No, Urmila! Your words make great sense. I can see that you were in deep meditation.'

'I knew, Akka, that you would understand. That's why I broke my silence today. But, Akka, if you ever have to face the kind of trial I did, do not respond in a predictable manner. Do not allow the situation to force you into mundaneness, into nastiness. Do not let it burn you up in anger, hatred. Save yourself. Assert your right over yourself. Give up your power over others. Then you will belong to yourself. You will be yourself. It's not easy to remain ourselves—trust me, Akka!'

As Urmila spoke, calm descended on Sita's heart. She knew that she would not be able to comprehend Urmila's experience of all these years in a single day. She relayed Urmila's words to Rama.

'I hope this power will not trouble my brother,' said Rama.

'All troubles seem to vanish in the presence of Urmila,' Sita said.

Every now and then Sita would go to Urmila, savour her words, her smile, her peace and her glow.

After Lakshmana left her in the forest, when Sita felt she had been abandoned in the middle of an ocean, Urmila appeared fleetingly before Sita's eyes.

When Sita was crying in the wilderness, asking if nothing but separation and rumours were her lot, she recalled Urmila's words.

Lakshmana followed Rama into the forest without informing Urmila.

Rama instructed Lakshmana to leave Sita in the forest without telling her anything.

Protest or penance, whatever it was, Urmila had saved herself.

Assume authority. Give up power. Then you'll belong to yourself. Then you'll be yourself. We should remain ourselves. Urmila had repeated these words many times in different ways. Those words had allayed Sita's concern for Urmila.

But was it her turn now to launch the protest? When would her anger abate? When would truth be realized? How?

Immense love and affection for Rama—how could she attain liberation from him?

What kind of a trial was this? The trial by fire was nothing compared to it! She was well versed in the art of warfare, but she had never waged a war against anyone. Now she had to wage a war against herself.

The battle had begun. How long was it going to continue?

'Ramachandra is performing Aswamedha Yaga, Sita. He has sent an invitation. I'll go, Amma,' Maharshi Valmiki said.

Maharshi waited for a while for Sita's response, then left. Sita did not notice his leaving. She was in no state to notice anything.

How can Rama perform the Aswamedha Yaga? Without her—his spouse—next to him?

Who was going to sit in her place?

A flame began to burn in Sita's heart.

'What does it matter? How does it concern you?' said Urmila, smiling as she walked in, as if she had read Sita's mind.

'Urmila!' Sita was taken by surprise.

'Yes, I've come. Lakshmana told me that you were here. I knew that the news of the Aswamedha Yaga would reach you. I could also imagine the storm the news would unleash in your heart. I have come to make sure that you remain yourself in this situation.'

Sita embraced Urmila and sat her down next to her. A long silence followed, and a lot was said in that silence. Then Sita asked, 'Is Rama himself performing the yaga?'

'Who else will do it? It's the emperor's prerogative, isn't it?'

'How will he do it without me?'

'Why should that question trouble you? If at all, it should occur to Rama. Or to those who are going to conduct the yaga. Isn't it foolish to get anxious about unnecessary things?' asked Urmila, as if she were older than Sita.

'You certainly know, Urmila. Tell me who is sitting with Rama in the yaga?'

'I have not come here to give you an answer that will either temporarily douse or further flare up the fire that is consuming you. I've come to tell you not to torture yourself with unnecessary questions.'

'But I am unable to swallow this.'

'Don't swallow. Don't even let it enter your mind. You must liberate yourself from Rama.'

'Urmila—'

Sita sobbed convulsively.

'How many tests and trials must I go through, Urmila?'

'Each of those trials is meant to liberate you from Rama. To secure you for yourself. Fight, meditate, look within until you find the truth that is you.'

'It's hard, sister.' The words came out of Sita's throat with great difficulty.

'It will be comforting, too, Akka. Try. I'll go now.' Urmila stood up.

'Why so soon? Don't you want to know about my children? Won't you see them?'

'I will, certainly, when they come to see me.'

Urmila left as suddenly as she had come. But the flames in Sita's heart were not doused so easily. Sparks of fire that lay buried in some corner, ash-covered embers dormant in her for a long time, began to blaze now. Just when Sita was getting used to the pleasure of those flames, she realized they had to be put out.

What was more enjoyable—loving Rama or being angry with him? Her mind oscillated endlessly in this dilemma.

It is not easy to ignite self-consuming anger or to stoke it. It is equally difficult to grasp the pleasure that passes off as sorrow.

It was also not easy to bear the sorrow that came out of the joy of loving Rama. Surmounting these dualities and liberating herself from Rama was proving to be arduous for Sita.

Yet Sita made the effort.

She continued to churn the stormy sea till it turned into an ocean of peace.

Gradually peace pervaded Sita.

By the time Valmiki returned from the Aswamedha Yaga, Sita's mind was completely at ease.

Who sat next to Rama to perform the yaga? It did not even occur to Sita to ask Valmiki the question.

After some days, Valmiki came to convey an important message to Sita.

'Rama has accepted Lava and Kusa. He has accepted Sita, too. But Sita must declare herself innocent in the open court.'

Sita listened calmly to these words. With a smile.

'Is there a need for me to do that?' That's all she said.

Liberated now from her children too, Sita, with a peaceful smile on her face, set out to return to where she had come from.

The Shackled

Rama's abode was in pitch darkness. No one had dared light a lamp.

No one had the courage to disturb Rama's solitude. The dark night wore on.

Though it was evident that Sita was no longer with Rama and that she would never return, the sun would still rise, the birds would sing, the flowers would bloom. That is the law of nature.

The laws of nature do not change. If they do, it will be calamitous for the world.

Human laws change. Human beings change them. Unable to cope with the change, they get perturbed. Slowly they get used to the change. Once the change stabilizes, they desire change again. Human law becomes the law of the time, and the law of the moment becomes the law of human beings. During the period of transition, the lives of the people who are key to the change go haywire.

Rama was in exactly such a situation now.

Since his childhood he had been entrusted by his teachers with the responsibility of preserving and propagating Arya Dharma.

They made him an expert in matters of the state, administration, royal responsibilities, governance and the duties of a kshatriya.

That very sense of duty was now slipping from Rama's throat into his heart. It tasted like poison.

When Shiva held poison in his throat, it benefitted the world, they said.

Unless Rama swallowed the poison, the world would not prosper, they said.

Rama swallowed.

Torture. Unbearable suffering.

Loneliness, terrible loneliness.

Except the time he spent playing with his brothers in childhood ....

But as childhood receded, an impregnable circle of power began to be drawn around him.

Except as a prince or as a future king, he was no longer seen as someone capable of familial attachments and affections.

As his teachers tightened their hold over him, he was distanced from everybody else. How to smile, how to walk, how long he should talk and to whom, what rites and rituals he should perform and how—what the duties of a king were, of a son, and of a kshatriya—what the history of his dynasty was, who the great men born in Raghu Vamsa were, what he should do as their heir—this line of thought gradually began to carry him along.

Lakshmana, too, stopped placing his hand on Rama's shoulder and began to greet him with folded hands. He stopped walking alongside Rama and started to walk a little behind him.

It was during this time, when Rama was getting distanced from everyone, including Lakshmana, that Sage Viswamitra arrived like an unsought boon and took him to the forest for a few days.

In the forest, he and Lakshmana once again walked hand in hand, laughed together and wandered around together, side by side.

Then—after that—like a gift from Creation, the daughter of Earth, Sita, became his spouse.

A rare and precious friend, a companion who dispelled his loneliness.

Sita, who would befriend him in their private chambers, free from the biddings of others, was like a goddess to him.

But soon began the exhortations that there were matters that should not be shared even with one's wife.

Boundaries were drawn for Sita as well.

So many ups and downs. So many trials and tribulations.

When everything appeared to have settled down,

and as he was exulting over his fatherhood that was in the offing—permanent separation from Sita.

As Rama recollected the course of events, his eyes turned into the petals of a blood-red lotus.

Lakshmana came and stood in front.

Both of them knew.

Lakshmana was back after leaving Sita in the forest and unburdening himself of the responsibility Rama had entrusted to him. But his heart was heavy like a ball of lead.

Both shed tears in silence.

'Anna! You're an emperor, you should not shed tears,' said Lakshmana, finding his voice with great effort.

'Don't I have the freedom even to grieve, Lakshmana? I know I am bound in chains, but tears can't be shackled. They are ripping open my iron heart and flowing out.' Unable to restrain himself, Lakshmana placed one hand on his brother's shoulder and wiped his tears with the other.

'Why is it unfolding this way, Rama?' Lakshmana's voice was filled with grief.

'It is impossible for it to happen in any other way. My life will have to lie suppressed under authority. Thanks to our mother, Kaikeyi, I could live in freedom with Sita for thirteen years in the forest. That's all.

'The time that I spent happily with Sita was indeed Kaikeyi's blessing to me. You don't know how indebted I am to her. She freed me from this throne and from authority. I was happy when I had to leave everything and go to the forest. Do you remember, Lakshmana?'

Lakshmana was astonished, even in his state of despair.

'Anna, are you grieving for yourself? I've just abandoned my vadina in the forest. I wonder what her fate is going to be.'

'Sita and I are inseparable, Lakshmana. None of you understand that. I am grieving for both of us. Nothing untoward will happen to her. She is the daughter of Earth. She is a strong and able woman. She will give birth to a good son and fully enjoy the pleasures of bringing him up. I am the one who is weak and incapable. My exalted nobleness is my handicap. With this political power, I have lost power over myself. I have lost my Sita. I have lost my son.'

Lakshmana did not have the strength to bear Rama's sorrow.

It is not in Rama's hands to give up his authority.

It is not Rama's sole discretion to give up his kingdom.

The day Rama prepared himself, joyously and without any apprehensions, to wear the crown, it left him. He did not even have the time to find out what forces had robbed him of the throne. Instead, he was overjoyed that he had got the opportunity to perform the noblest duty of a son in Arya Dharma, to honour his father's word. Before Rama set out for the forest, Vasista explained to him gently:

'Rama, you're an heir to Raghu Vamsa. You're giving up your kingdom for fourteen years. That doesn't mean you are giving up your dharma as a king, as a kshatriya. Remember the promise you made to Parasurama at the time of your marriage to Sita. Spread Arya Dharma over the entire southern plain. The entire world should become an Aryan Empire.'

Rama recollected everything.

He recalled the agreement he had made with Parasurama, the slayer of kshatriyas, before he entered into wedlock with Sita.

On the day of the wedding, Parasurama arrived blazing with anger. At the time, Rama was lost in chanting Sita's name, unaware of everything else. Sita, Janaki, Vaidehi, Mythili—each of her names rained nectar in his heart. At the sight of her face faintly visible from behind the veil, Rama felt himself afloat like the soft mountain breeze. For the first time he experienced a state of unburdened joy.

Breaking Shiva's bow, Sita adorning his neck with a garland, everything happened as if in a dream.

Rama was in no position to talk to Parasurama. So the elders intervened.

Who did not know of Parasurama's valour or vengeance, and his vow to exterminate every kshatriya from the face of the Earth?

All the great sages—Brahmarshis and Rajarshis—held negotiations with Parasurama. They sent for Rama too.

'If Rama makes a promise to firmly establish Arya Dharma in the southern as well as the northern plains, the marriage of Rama and Sita may take place,' Parasurama said bluntly.

'I do know Arya Dharma. Sages like Vasista have trained me in it. It has been implemented in our kingdom,' Rama said politely.

'It should be implemented more rigorously, more widely and with greater dedication.' Dasaratha promised on behalf of Rama, lest the latter say something that would annoy Parasurama.

When Rama was about to say something, Parasurama interjected—'Honouring one's father's word is the noblest deed in Arya Dharma. Comply with that first.'

Everybody fell silent.

After Parasurama was pacified, Rama and Sita's wedding took place without any further hindrance.

Vasista reminded him of all this as Rama was setting out for his fourteen-year sojourn in the forest.

As he was reminded of the past, memories of his life in the forest entered Rama's thoughts like peacocks with their tails spread out. The first thirteen years of forest life were the most pleasurable years of his life. Those were the years of love that he had spent with Sita. The cool breeze blowing across the river, the intoxicating forest fragrances, the romance that flourished amidst the cooings of various birds. Those were the days when he had securely hidden Sita behind his eyelids. Those were the days when he took delight in Sita's lap, indulging in love play. He had nothing much to do in those days, except to slay a few non-Aryans and spread Arya Dharma among the sages living there. That was the time when he was free from the customary guardedness and caution of the court and the palace. That was the time when he and Sita were like two lovebirds lost in each other's company. That was the time when they chased each other like a pair of deer. The rising of the moon, the twinkling of stars, the blooming of flowers, the blowing of the breeze—everything was just for the two of them—Rama and Sita. The brooks frolicked only because Rama and Sita bathed in them. The woods would affectionately take them into their lap and indulge them in their playfulness.

Even in those times, he used to get occasional instructions from Ayodhya. About the expansion of the Aryan Empire. About the indispensability of friendship with Sugriva and enmity with Ravana. Let the opportune time come, Rama thought. The opportune time did come the day Surpanakha appeared. That day he discharged his rajadharma—his duty as a king. To provoke an enemy—an enemy who is to be conquered—

into battle, is the rightful duty of an Aryan king. The opportunity presented itself in the form of Surpanakha. By humiliating his sister, Ravana could be drawn into a direct battle, thought Rama, who had little experience in administering a kingdom.

But Ravana was adept at statecraft and military strategies. He was not a novice to cross the seas with his army and fight a war on alien soil. Instead, he abducted Sita—Rama's beloved. Ravana thought Rama would not be able to cross the seas and win a war in a foreign land where he had no foothold. But Rama had the strength to cross not one but seven seas for Sita's sake. Perhaps Ravana did not know this.

Whether he knew it not, Ravana paid the price. But even before he was slain, there were whispers in the air. Whether it was in keeping with Arya Dharma to bring Sita back to Ayodhya.

But to return to Ayodhya without Sita! That was unthinkable for Rama. He had not fought an entire war just to show off the prowess of the Aryan Empire. It was for Sita. Even if no one else believed it, he thought Sita would.

But should he take Sita to Ayodhya and humiliate her in front of everybody?

Must Sita listen to all that they would say?

If Sita were to be asked to prove her chastity before the people of Ayodhya, would she be able to bear it?

But unless Sita's chastity was proved, the royal court of Ayodhya would not welcome her with respect and cordiality.

He knew that very well. So he thought it should be resolved in Lanka itself.

Trial by fire—for his Sita.

For his sake, for his sake alone, did Sita, a woman of dignity, agree to it.

He had thought that he would have no option but to fall at Sita's feet and beg forgiveness for subjecting her to the ignominy.

But Sita understood his situation. She decided to protect him and his worldly and kingly duties. She wanted to assure him that she was there for him.

She hid the seas of humiliation and grief behind her eyelids, and came forth unperturbed like a pot of water and doused the fire.

'Don't forgive me, Sita—' he held back the words behind his lips. Her lips delicately brushed away those words.

All is well, he thought innocently.

But a shadow of sadness had already gathered in Sita's eyes. He knew Sita had sustained a wound for his sake. He thought he would be able to heal that wound with his love and with the miraculous power of time. Today, he cut open that wound again, left it incurable and abandoned her.

He caused her heart to bleed incessantly for her humiliation.

A wound that would never heal.

A wound that would hurt every day.

A wound caused by the throne to the love of Sita and Rama.

He could forsake Sita; Sita belonged to him.

He could not relinquish the throne; it belonged to Raghu Vamsa.

The dynasty. The tradition in which political power passes on to the firstborn. The dharma of preserving that tradition was on his head. The burden of protecting Arya Dharma finally robbed him of all the happiness in his life.

There was no liberation for him.

Rama wailed disconsolately.

Having heard that two young monks from the forest were singing the saga of Rama, Lakshmana wanted to present them before Rama.

But meeting Rama was difficult now even for Lakshmana.

Rama was an emperor. He occupied the throne. Wore the crown.

Except for the throne and the crown, he paid no attention to anything else. He had no other interest either.

To mothers, brothers, relatives—to every one of them—he was Emperor Ramachandra.

Had Rama changed into a machine in order to forget the pain of separation from Sita? Or had he sent Sita away to the forest knowing he would inevitably have to turn into a mechanical being once he took over the reins of power, and that Sita would not be able to bear the change in him? Lakshmana and Anjaneya often wondered about this.

They waited to see him smile but they did not know that there was a permanent rift between authority and an affectionate smile.

A kingdom had to be governed. And for governance one needed blunt weapons. Only those carried any value.

Lakshmana thought that Rama's heart might melt at the sight of those hermit boys.

Their songs were sweet; their faces were sweet; their words were sweet. The nectar of their voices might be the right medicine to melt Rama's heart, which had turned to stone, thought Lakshmana.

Rama listened to his brother's words disinterestedly.

They could sing the saga of Rama. But what did they know of the saga of the Rama bound by the shackles of power? Knowing nothing about it, what could they sing?

When Rama was a child, he had demanded the moon. He was shown a reflection of the moon in a mirror and was pacified. The boys could perhaps sing of that episode.

Rama was now bound to the throne and could not even insist that he wanted Sita. Could they sing that story?

They could sing beautifully of the wedding of Sita and Rama. But could they sing the story of Rama languishing in the agony of being permanently separated from Sita?

They would sing about Rama, the slayer of the demon king Ravana. But could those young boys sing of the Rama who extinguished all traces of love within himself?

As Rama's face turned pale, Lakshmana lost all hope.

'Anna, please heed my words, just this one time. Their singing will be like a balm to your burning heart.'

'Heart? My heart? Burning?'

'Their songs will be like cool nectar to your blazing mind.'

'Mind? My mind? I who execute the Arya Dharma without a second thought, do I have a mind of my own?'

'Anna, for my sake—'

Lakshmana fell at Rama's feet.

Rama nodded in consent.

Lava and Kusa approached Rama, seated in the royal court amidst his distinguished courtiers, and greeted him with folded hands. Rama was moved the moment he saw them. Clearly they were his reflections. Princes in the guise of hermits. Everything became clear to Rama. He drew them close and embraced them. Everything was crystal clear to all the courtiers as well. In the discussion on dharma that followed, it was resolved that Rama could accept his sons.

'What about Sita?'

The debate about dharma started all over again.

'If Sita declares her innocence in the court, Ramachandra may accept her.'

Valmiki left for his ashram with this news.

But Rama knew Sita would never come back.

Giving him his sons, the joy of their embrace—she had saved him, as always.

She thawed the stone that Rama's heart had turned into. She made the withered plant sprout again.

He too, as always, left Sita to more sorrow. Like a wild beast stamping on a tender creeper every time it tried to rise with the help of some prop or the other, he destroyed Sita's desire to live every time she nurtured it.

Sita was not coming back into his life. She would entrust the children to him and liberate herself. But he could not find liberation until he turned them into heirs to Raghu Vamsa.

But by giving him his sons, Sita had cleared the way for his liberation. She had always stood by him. She had always protected him. In Ayodhya, everyone swore by Rama's protection.

Who knew that Sita was Sri Rama's protective charm?

Sita Herself Can Save Us
Volga

Forging a Vision of Liberation
T. Vijay Kumar and C. Vijayasree

Volga: An Interview
T. Vijay Kumar

P.S.

Insights
Interviews
& More...

Sita Herself Can Save Us

Volga

© Bharath Bhushan

The stories in this collection revolve around the character of Sita against the backdrop of the Ramayana. It was perhaps Tripuraneni Ramaswamy Chowdhury[1] who, in the last century, started the trend of rewriting stories from [Hindu] mythology. Rama's slaying of the Shudra ascetic Shambuka under the influence of Brahmin hegemony, and acting on their complaint, is presented in the Ramayana as an act of protecting dharma. But in *Shambuka Vadha*, Tripuraneni exposed the injustice and made us rethink what caste has to do with performing penance. Times change, and along with it change customs and traditions. Dharmas of the past become meaningless and unjust now. To convey this truth, many writers continue to rethink and rewrite stories from mythology. Going a step further, Chalam[2] reconfigured mythological characters from a rationalist perspective. He presented Sita who saw Ravana as someone who ruined himself for her sake to be a truer lover than Rama. She in fact enters the funeral pyre of Ravana. Chalam also wrote many stories and plays presenting in a humourous way Harishchandra's truthfulness, Prahlad's devotion to Vishnu, and Kuchela's progeny. In plays like *Pururava* and *Shashanka*, he critiqued contemporary morals and the ways of the world through mythological characters, to create awareness that we should overcome narrow boundaries and egos. In the story 'Ashoka Vanam', KoKu[3] wonders at the cruelty of burning down the Ashoka garden. In 'Jambavantha's Dream', he introduced revolutionary thoughts into Jambavanth's character.

I suppose these examples are enough to show that using characters from mythology is an established practice in Telugu literature. Since the characters are already known to the reader, the author is spared of the effort to introduce them, and can then concentrate on the subject. Among the stories here, I wrote 'The Reunion' first. I was inspired to write it by a scene in my dance–drama *War and Peace*. Declaring that they are not the cause of the battle between Rama and Ravana, Sita and Surpanakha sing and dance together:

Desire to expand the Aryan Empire
Ignited the Rama–Ravana war

It's an Arya–Dravida clash
Women too became pawns.

At first, Sita and Surpanakha sing separately that they are lovers of peace and pastoral life, worshippers of beauty, yet could not escape insults, suspicions and humiliations. Later, they dance together to the above song. The audience appreciated it a great deal. Surpanakha's character received a lot of compliments. But there were some doubts too. Firstly, and importantly, in the dancers themselves. The Surpanakha they knew was a demon. The Surpanakha I portrayed claims to be a worshipper of beauty and a friendly and loving person. The dancers therefore were hesitant to play such a character. They were convinced only after it was explained to them that Surpanakha was a Dravidian woman, and that the traditions and customs of the Dravidians were different from those of the Aryans, and that the Dravidians were depicted as demons in the Puranas. They then represented the character aesthetically. But several questions came up when the dance–drama was to be telecast on Doordarshan. They could not see Surpanakha as anything but a demon. They were used to understanding the suffering of Sita and Draupadi, but how could one place Surpanakha by their side? What did Surpanakha suffer in the first place? She got punished for lusting after an unknown man. Other than that, what was her distress? In fact, aren't Sita and Surpanakha rivals? How can they dance together? Such questions were posed, and those at Doordarshan were not satisfied with our answers. Eventually they censored Surpanakha's role before telecasting it.

That's when I felt like writing a story about Surpanakha's pain. I wondered why Sita and Surpanakha could not be friends. The result was the story 'Reunion'. In this story, Sita notices

Surpanakha's deep insight. She notes Surpanakha's empowerment and Surpanakha's struggle with herself to achieve it.

After writing the story, I felt great affection for Sita's character. Sita, who loved Rama so much and received so much love from him, was subjected to insults and scorn by the same man. Sita who would ensconce herself in the loving embrace of Rama, Sita who would walk in the footsteps of Rama—she rejected the same man, even deserted her children and followed her own path. Her experiences pushed her in that direction. However, I felt that there must have been other women who joined Sita in her journey. Sita must have struggled hard with herself to leave Rama. Merely being angry with him would not have been enough to separate herself from him. Psychoanalysts say that anger and hatred tie people together. More than love, anger and malice bind people to each other rather than liberate them. Therefore, Sita did not leave in anger. She left with a matured mind. I felt that her maturity may have come from her worldly experience. She must have internalized the strength that she got from outside. There were many women before her—in the Ramayana itself—who were victims of insults, rejections, curses and neglect by the world, families and husbands. Ahalya came to my mind first. The story 'The Music of the Earth' was written with the idea of a meeting between Ahalya and Sita.

What Renuka and Urmila had to experience was not any less. If they share their experiences, knowledge and wisdom with Sita, perhaps it would add further strength to her. Such cooperation among women is an idea dear to me and these stories are infused with it. These stories also represent women's suffering in contemporary society. While some women overcome the restrictions, insults and violence they are subjected to, many others remain trapped, unable to escape, and unaware of the need to escape. Women who are unaware of the need to liberate themselves from abusive husbands continue to hang on to them even while loathing them. Women are used to inflicting violence upon themselves out of hatred.

These stories are for such women.

Ramadasu[4] sang *'Plead with the lord to save me, O Mother Sita'.* I believe that the Sita of these stories does not need to plead with anyone—she herself can save us.

'Who will save us?' asked Tyagayya.[5] I hope these stories will gives us the confidence to answer 'We ourselves'. With these stories I have made five dear friends: Sita, Surpanakha, Ahalya, Renuka and Urmila. I am confident that these friends of mine will give my fellow women strength, courage and wisdom.

Notes

1. Popularly known as Kaviraju, Tripuraneni Ramaswamy (1887 –1943) was a lawyer, poet, playwright and reformer. He is considered the first poet to introduce rationalism and humanism into Telugu poetry and literature.
2. Gudipati Venkata Chalam (1894–1979) is one of the most influential writers in modern Telugu literature. Bold, women-centric themes, unconventional narrative technique and a philosophical outlook characterize his writing.
3. Kodavatiganti Kutumba Rao (1909–1980), an important writer in Telugu, was a firm believer in the social purpose of literature.
4. Kancherla Gopanna (c 1620–1680), popularly known as Bhakta Ramadasu or Bhadrachala Ramadasu, was a devotee of Rama and a composer of Carnatic music. He is one among the famous *vaggeyakaras* (a person who composes the lyrics and also sets them to music) in Telugu. The reference here is to his famous *keertana 'Nanu brovamani cheppave seethamma thalli ...'*.

5. Kakarla Tyagabrahmam (1767–1847), popularly known as Tyagayya in Telugu, is one of the greatest composers of Carnatic music. He composed thousands of devotional songs, mostly in praise of Rama, including the famous *pancharatna kritis* ('five jems'). The reference here is to his *kriti 'Brochevarevarura ...'*.

Translated from the Telugu by T. Vijay Kumar

Forging a Vision of Liberation

T. Vijay Kumar and C. Vijayasree

Volga's *Vimukta*, translated as *The Liberation of Sita*, is a slim collection of five stories. All of them draw on the Ramayana and have Sita as the principal character. Each story is independent and yet connected. In each of them Sita learns a lesson that facilitates her liberation. Interestingly, it is the minor characters in Valmiki's epic—Surpanakha, Renuka, Urmila and Ahalya—who occupy centre stage and assume a major role in educating Sita. The title story signals Sita's emergence as the liberated one while the final story, 'The Shackled', shows Rama imprisoned in the bondage of Arya Dharma.

What Volga attempts through these stories is a compelling exercise in 're-visionist myth-making'. It was nearly four decades ago that Adrienne Rich made that famous statement about women's writing as 're-visioning'. In the words of Rich, 'Re-vision—the act of looking back, of seeing with fresh eyes, of entering an old text from a new critical direction—is for us [women] more than a chapter in cultural history, it is an act of survival' (18). Since then, re-visioning has figured prominently on the agenda of women writers, and all institutions—political, social and religious—have been subjected to a critical re-vision in women's writing. Even the processes of cognition and contemplation have not escaped the re-visionist project and feminism has come to mean 'a rethinking of thinking' itself (Held, 60). In the process, re-vision no longer remains a simple act of looking back nor a mere act of survival. It evolves into an active remaking of the past and a re-invention of tradition. In other words, re-vision has turned into an act of creation and trans-creation.

As part of this remaking of the past, old stories—stories from ancient myths—came to be retold in new ways, from gynocentric perspectives. Women initially tried to make an intervention into myths and subsequently acquired the confidence to play with them. As Patricia Yaegar points out, 'As women play with old texts, the burden of tradition is lightened and shifted; it has the potential of being remade' (18).This playful reinvention of myths has figured prominently in Indian women's writing as well. Mahasweta Devi's 'Dopdi' and 'Stanadayani' (Bangla), Yashodhara Mishra's 'Purana Katha' (Odiya), Muppala Ranganayakamma's *Ramayana Visha Vrikham* (Telugu), Sara Joseph's *Ramayana Kathakal* (Malayalam)—to name a few, exemplify this trend. Through their retellings, women not only break the hold of tradition but free tradition from its fixity and take it to a free zone where multiple mutations and transmutations become possible.

Volga's *Vimukta* not only belongs to this tradition of feminist revisionist myth-making but takes it further. Volga does not use re-visioning merely as a strategy to subvert patriarchal structures embedded in mythical texts but also as a means to forge a vision of life in which liberation is total, autonomous and complete. She also creates a community of women by re-presenting myths from alternative points of view, and by networking women across ages and generations. She achieves this through different narrative strategies: giving voice to women characters marginalized in the 'master narrative', extending the story of a character beyond its conventional closure; forging female bonds and creating a female collective; and redefining many conventional epistemes including liberation.

'The Reunion' narrates the story of Sita meeting Surpanakha in the forest. Sita, abandoned by Rama, takes refuge in Valmiki's ashram and devotes herself to raising her sons. She meets Surpanakha, who, after her humiliation and mutilation, has recovered and creates for herself a state of ineffable joy by cultivating a beautiful garden. Surpanakha, having conquered her rage and revenge, realizes that beauty is not a physical attribute but the truth of nature. She finds fulfillment in growing a garden that reflects the beauty of nature. Having attained a state of non-dependent joy, she also finds a soulmate in Sudhira who respects her wisdom and discernment. Sita learns that her fulfillment, too, does not lie in bringing up her children but in discovering herself. She tells Surpanakha, 'After my children leave me and go to the city, I will become the daughter of Mother Earth. Resting under these cool trees, I shall create a new meaning for my life.' Thus Sita and Surpanakha strike a bond of sisterhood not as victims of patriarchy but as two mature women in pursuit of self-realization.

'The Music of the Earth' is a retelling of Ahalya's story. The popular version of Ahalya's story portrays her as a victim of patriarchal norms of female chastity. Lord Indra, desirous of her beauty, dons the form of Ahalya's husband, Sage Gautama and enjoys her. The sage, on coming to know of this, curses Indra and turns Ahalya into a boulder. Later, he provides relief by telling her that she would be redeemed from her accursed state by the touch of the holy feet of Sri Rama. In Volga's story, Ahalya meets

Sita in the forest and enlightens her about the complexities in popular notions of female chastity. According to Ahalya, the core issue is not that of female fidelity or the lack of it but of man's power to put it to test. Sita does not understand the implication of this argument until she is asked to face the trial by fire. She recalls Ahalya's words when she is asked to prove her chastity by going through the fire test, yet she brushes it off convincing herself that it is not out of suspicion that Rama has put her chastity to test. However, when Sita is abandoned by Rama, Ahalya visits her in Valmiki's ashram. Now Sita is able to appreciate Ahalya's astuteness and listens to her advice intently: 'Don't grieve over what has already happened. It is all for your own good, and is part of the process of self-realization. Be happy. Observe nature and the evolution of life. Notice the continual changes in them … You belong to this whole world, not just to Rama …'

Renuka, the wife of Sage Jamadagni, whom her own son Parasurama beheads in obedience to his father's injunction, is the spokesperson of the story, 'The Sand Pot'. She tells Sita how paativratyam or fidelity of a married woman is as fragile as a sand pot. A fleeting feeling of desire for a gandharva makes her an adulteress in the eyes of her husband who then orders their son to behead her. No woman can escape a charge of this kind. It is, therefore, futile for a woman to anchor her identity in her marital status or in her motherhood. Though Sita doesn't follow Renuka's advice initially, it proves useful to Sita when the time comes to hand over her grown up sons to Rama. Rama gives Sita the opportunity to return to the royal household on the condition that she declares her innocence in the royal court. But her question is: 'Do I need to do that? Is there any sense to such an effort?' Instead she chooses to join her mother—Mother Earth.

'The Liberated' offers the interesting account of an encounter between Sita, who returns to the royal household after fourteen years of life in the forest, and Urmila, who lives all those years in a self-imposed penance. Urmila, breaking her fourteen-year long silence, tells Sita how she felt abandoned and dejected when her husband left her to accompany Rama into the forest. Out of annoyance and rage, she withdrew into a self-imposed exile within the four walls of her chambers but that wrath slowly turned into a quest for truth. She began to study herself, her feelings, her emotions and her relationships. She saw how love, hate, jealousy and respect are but shades of the same condition—dependence on others. She struggled with all these and arrived at a state of inner peace. Sita finds Urmila's experience edifying. Later in Valmiki's ashram, when Sita comes to know that Rama is performing the Aswamedha Yaga, she feels terribly disturbed by the thought that Rama might have taken another wife to become eligible to perform the ritual. Urmila visits her sister in that hour of despair and makes Sita realize that it is immaterial whether Rama takes another wife or not. She tells Sita: 'You must liberate yourself from Rama … Each of these trials is meant to liberate you from Rama. To secure you for yourself. Fight, meditate, look within until you find the truth that is you.' Liberation from Rama marks the real emancipation for Sita.

'The Shackled', the last story in the collection, reads like an extended interior monologue of Rama. Held captive in the prison of Arya Dharma, Rama has no personal freedom. The only time Rama could just be himself was the period of his banishment in the forest, which to him was more of a boon since it freed him from the rigid frames of royal power. Rama confesses to Lakshmana: 'My exalted nobleness is my handicap. With this political power, I have lost power over myself. I have lost my Sita. I have lost my son.' At every stage Rama remains chained to Arya Dharma. Eventually, when Sita hands over the children to Rama as heirs to his throne, she liberates herself. But Rama remains shackled.

Volga's re-visionist myth-making thus opens new spaces within the old discourse, enabling women to view their life and experiences from gynocentric perspectives. They recreate a world of freedom in which they not only willingly bear the responsibility of their own survival, but also have a sense of joy and complete freedom. Women are no longer means to serve someone else's ends, nor are they merely the prizes in men's quests. On the contrary, they are questers seeking their own salvation.

Works cited

Held, Virginia. *The Ethics of Care: Personal, Political, and Global.* New York: OUP, 2006. Print.

Rich, Adrienne. 'When We Dead Awaken: Writing as Re-Vision'. *College English* 34.1, 'Women, Writing and Teaching' (1972): 18–30. Print.

Yaeger, Patricia. *Honey-Mad Women: Emancipatory Strategies in Women's Writing.* NY: Columbia University Press, 1988. Print.

Volga: An Interview

T. Vijay Kumar

'Volga' is the name by which Popuri Lalitha Kumari (1950–) writes. 'Volga' was in fact the name of her elder sister who died an untimely death when Lalitha Kumari was sixteen. Their communist father had named her sister in memory of a Soviet girl who was killed by the Nazi Army on the same day her sister was born. After the death of her sister, Lalitha Kumari assumed her sister's name and to this day continues to write under the name Volga.

In her college days, Volga was an active member of the Students' Federation of India (SFI) and later joined the Revolutionary Writers' Association which was an offshoot of CPI (ML) (Communist Party of India-Marxist Leninist). Then in 1980, frustrated by the party's patriarchal attitude towards women, she quit left politics and devoted herself to propagate feminism among Telugu readers through her activism and writing.

Among Volga's nearly fifty publications are seven novels, six short story collections, nine edited volumes, twelve translations from English, six books of literary criticism and three feminist theoretical works.

T. Vijay Kumar: ***Which is your favourite genre and why?***

Volga: Short story and literary criticism. In a short story, you can convey what you want to concisely and with density. Short story has greater reach—it reaches more number of people—and is also perhaps relatively easier to write. I don't mean it is a 'light' genre, not by any means. It has its own complexities—you have to say everything in the limited space and you have to establish the characters within the limited canvas. But still, I like the short story. Whenever something appeals to me, I feel like writing a [short] story and not, say, a poem. Initially I did write poetry and then novels in a line. But later, I wrote more short stories. I also like literary criticism—not purely academic criticism but literary appreciation. Analyzing a book I liked from a feminist perspective gives me a lot of satisfaction.

What have been the influences on you as a writer?

In poetry, Sri Sri[1], Tilak[2] among others. When I started writing, Digambara Kavulu[3] (Naked Poets) had created a stir in Telugu literature with their views and style. Influenced by them, I along with four other friends formed Paigambara Kavulu (Prophet-Poets) and brought out two anthologies. In fiction, Chalam[4] and KoKu[5] have been great influences. There has been no major women's writing tradition, and so I did not have any women writers as my role models. There certainly were women writers—like Malathi Chandur (1930–2013), for instance—but because of my political outlook, they did not appeal to me. They may have been role models for others, but to me, influenced as I was by revolutionary writers like Sri Sri, their concerns—family and domestic matters—looked too limited.

When did you shift from writing poetry to writing fiction, and why?

When I was in college, I wrote a poem titled 'Panchadi Nirmala varasuraalini' ('I am the heir of Panchadi Nirmala',[6] 1972). It got me a lot of recognition, perhaps more than any other work of mine. Then I wrote a short story—'Jailu gadi aatmakatha' ('Autobiography of a prison cell', 1972)—while I was a member of the Revolutionary Writers Association. That story gave me a lot of satisfaction, if not recognition. I felt that I found my medium. It was a sort of self-discovery, and I felt more capable writing short stories than poetry. I thought that the story came out exactly as I had conceived it, which was not often the case in poetry. Later, too, I wrote a few stories which were received quite well.

If writing gave you such satisfaction, why was there a break in your writing career?

Yes, there was a long gap in my writing career and it was because of my activism. I was doing a lot of work in the Revolutionary Writers Association and in the civil liberties movement. That work took most of my time and precedence over writing because, while there were many others who were writing, there weren't many at that time to do the kind of work I was willing to do. Moreover, I was writing at a time when there were stalwarts—Sri Sri, RaaVi Sastry[7], KoKu, KV Ramana Reddy (1928–1998)—who were all my seniors in RWA. Then my colleagues and immediate seniors were Varavara Rao,[8] Tiragabadda Kavulu, Cherabanda Raju[9] and other Digambara Kavulu. There were no women, unfortunately. Only Krishna Bai used to come, but she was not a creative writer but an occasional critic and was much senior to me. I was, thus, in the company of well-established and dynamic writers. So I thought that since so many of them were writing—and so well—nothing would be lost if I didn't write. I was, therefore, more into organizing meetings, rallies, signature campaigns—against the Emergency (1975–77), for instance—which took all my time.

So where do you stand in the debate between art and activism?

The reason for my not writing for a while was not because I considered literature less important. Not at all! Thanks to my father, there were always good books at home. I started reading very good literature from the age of seven. So I grew up on literature and firmly believed that literature was a powerful medium, and that it can change people and society. In fact, I used to have even greater illusions then. But there were so many writers producing such good work. However, there were no women activists. To work with women, to mobilize them—I felt that I was needed more there. So it was only the dearth of women in activism that drew me away from writing and was not my lack of faith in the importance of literature.

But then you left activism and came back to writing.

Yes, there certainly were different phases in my writing career. Before the 1980s, I was a writer, but a non-serious one. I was more inclined towards activism. Then in 1981, I quit left politics and turned to feminist politics. It was a turning point in my career. I took writing seriously as I felt obliged to write because no one was writing about feminism or from feminist perspectives in Telugu. So to introduce feminism and to take it to the people, I felt I had to write. Writing is a powerful medium, and in any case, it was the only option available to me then as there were no major feminist movements. So in 1983, I started with literary criticism and published *Athadu, aame, manam* (*He, She, We*),[10] which explained how to read a text from a feminist point of view.

Then since 1985, I have been writing novels and short stories regularly. So one can say that, in my writing career, the pre-1980s was the leftist phase and the post-80s was the feminist phase.

How has your understanding of feminism evolved over time?

When I started in the '80s, reading and writing at a feverish pace, I looked at women as a homogeneous category—that all women were one, a sort of 'workers of the world unite' kind of understanding. Then in the 1990s, caste emerged as a major issue—maybe because of the Karamchedu incident[11] and the debates that followed. I wrote *Aakasamlo sagam* (*Half the Sky*, 1990), with a Dalit heroine, and with the sense that all women are not the same and that caste plays a major role. Yet, when I did an anthology of feminist poetry *Neeli Meghalu* (*Blue Clouds*) in 1993, there weren't many Dalit women writers in it. There were, in fact, not many of them writing then with a Dalit-feminist consciousness. Yet, I felt that it was a shortcoming of the anthology. Gradually I realized the broad scope of feminism which includes not just caste, but also several other factors—religion, race, gender (LGBT). Feminism has given me that power to accept, understand and integrate differences. The inclusiveness that I learnt from feminism—I try to express in my writings.

What then is your response to the politics of representation?

I have been clear about it from the beginning. It is not right to say that only women should write about women. While I do believe that women can write about women's experiences better and differently because it is their own, I don't agree that only women should write. Such a stand is also unnatural. Without Gurajada[12], Chalam, KoKu—and if I hadn't read and understood them—I wouldn't be what I am today. Any human being who understands the suffering and the oppression of fellow beings can write about them. Even my first book of literary criticism *Athadu, aame, manam* was highly appreciative of Uppala Lakshmana Rao's novel. I also wrote research essays on Chalam, KoKu, etc. So I had that clarity from the beginning—that I do not agree that only women should write about women or only Dalits should write about Dalits. But gradually, because of the growing trend of exclusivism, my writing on Dalit issues has come down. This is because what I wrote was not only failing its purpose but was also creating unnecessary conflicts, and was leading to unconstructive and needless discussions—about authenticity, about what has not been included, etc. So if someone like me, who believes that anyone with the right understanding can write about Dalit issues, has reduced writing about them, I suppose it is even more so in the case of others.

Is non-Dalits not writing about Dalit issues a loss to the overall understanding of the issues?

It's a loss, definitely. Whatever I know, even if it is only little, I will want to share it, in my own way and in my own style, with my readers. But if I desist from doing so to avoid a needless controversy, it is definitely a loss. But it's not just in my case. There are many others who can write better than me. Take the case of [Akkineni] Kutumba Rao who wrote *Sorajjem* (*Self-government*) in 1981. After *Malapalli* (1922)[13] it is only the second Dalit novel in Telugu. It's a very good novel. There has been no novel after *Malapalli* which depicts Dalit life so effectively and so realistically. He could write it only because the current trend [of exclusivism] was not there then. I doubt if he can write it now. And if he can't, because of any apprehensions, isn't it a loss? It leaves a gap in the overall understanding because the non-Dalit perspective on caste is also a part of the total picture. How you perceive Dalit issues, from your upper caste perspective—whether you show sympathy, empathy, incomprehension or confusion—is also important. Isn't it better if that perspective is presented too? This atmosphere that inhibits such a representation is a little painful. Of course, Dalits should write, women should write. Everyone should write their own stories, there is no two ways about it. And they can write well too because subjective experience is always a powerful factor in writing.

Do you think the rise of identity movements is a blow to ideological movements?

Ideological movements had reached a stage where if they did not receive that blow, they would have been totally destroyed. That blow was needed and timely. It did not happen accidentally. Identity movements rose out of indifference, neglect. It is true that identity movements created splits initially, and women, Dalits, minorities separated. But I think such separation helps them to know their own identity, strengths and weaknesses. This process will take some time. But perhaps after that they will again arrive at a common identity. Oppression, for instance, is a common factor since all these movements were born out of oppression. Arriving at an understanding of what is common among their different oppressions may take a long time, but because of technology it might also take a very short time. But whatever is happening now, I feel, is for the good. Let everything come out—even if it is hatred, even if it is hatred arising out of misunderstanding, let everything that has accumulated over centuries come out. Once it has all cleared up, then there will be a realization of your true self. Then the atmosphere will become clearer. I'm optimistic.

Ideological movements encourage you to rise above the limitations of the self and see yourself as part of the larger group. Identity movements, on the other hand, are focused on the self. How can they come together?

Identity movements too are group-based. When women and Dalits are reduced to miniatures in the larger picture, there is a need to look at them up cose. Ideological movements overlooked them, and out of that neglect emerged identity movements. When the marginalized are seen closely, the picture that emerges will also be seen by the ideological groups and then perhaps there will be an interaction between the two.

What are your views on translation? How can translations become a bridge between the familiar and the strange?

Translations are very necessary. It was translated Soviet literature I read at a young age that shaped my perspective. I could arrive at some understanding of the wider world, of exploitation even at a young age. If I had read only our magazines and what contemporary women writers [in Telugu] were writing, my understanding would have been very limited. I wouldn't have been as politically aware at that young age of fourteen or fifteen. Later when I started translating, I did it with the conviction that those works needed to reach our readers. The essence of human experience is the same everywhere—pain, love, suffering, exploitation, struggle. But how does it work in different backgrounds? What is common among all these experiences? These are the interesting aspects of translation. For instance, the Russian context may be totally different, but a mother is a mother, anywhere.[14] So when I see a similarity between that mother and my mother, I feel happy. When I realize that the feeling called 'mother' is the same all over the world, my happiness is doubled.

Why is there a huge asymmetry between translations into Telugu and translations from it?

The asymmetry is very true. Very few of our works have been translated into other [Indian] languages. Nobody outside [the state] knows about our writers, even about the great ones like Sri Sri, Chalam, KoKu. To tell you the truth, as far as I know, few other Indian languages have writers like Sri Sri or Chalam. There was no one in the 1920s who wrote novels like [Chalam's] *Sasirekha* (1921) or *Maidaanam* (1927). Similarly a poem like [Sri Sri's] 'Kavita o kavita' is very rare in any Indian language literature. As Sri Sri once said in a poem, 'Andhraness is my curse'[15]. Maybe the Telugu people have a poor opinion about themselves and so they don't come forward to get their works translated. Speaking from my own experience—some of my works have been translated into Kannada, Marathi and Hindi. I don't usually try to get translated and am quite satisfied with writing for readers in my own language. But I really wanted at least a few of my stories translated into Malayalam, Bengali and Tamil, but it still hasn't happened!

Why are Telugu works not getting translated into English, then?

Publishing is the main hurdle. There are only a few publishers who publish translations. Moreover, there are several other issues: Who will do it? Who knows both languages well? How do you get to know of them or contact them? How to get it published? Very few Telugu writers think about all this. Unlike our writers, writers in other languages promote themselves well. Also, in other languages, those who know the language and are well versed in English promote their writers with zeal. In Telugu, there is no such zeal, I must say. Take your own example. Till you [and Vijayasree] translated *Kanyasulkam*, nobody thought about it although it is an acknowledged modern classic[16]. A few years ago, when [Alladi] Uma and [M] Sridhar translated my book[17] and invited me to speak at its launch, I felt so guilty the whole day! In hindsight, I feel that I may have hurt them, but I did not say anything about the book as I felt a little embarrassed that my book was translated into English when books of Gurajada, Chalam and KoKu were not! But, by and large, I have to say that there isn't much awareness in Telugu of the whole process of translation.

Self-publishing seems to be the norm in Telugu. Is it a sign of impatience or is it happening because there are no publishers? What is the publishing scene in Telugu?

There were many publishers during the 1960s when women were writing serials. There were many writers and readers, and the reading culture was strong. It disappeared in the '80s due to various reasons like the spread of English education, television, etc. At the same time, good writing was displaced by popular and pulp fiction. The whole scene became murky and publishers stopped publishing. So everyone started publishing their own books, which means there is no appraisal. But even before that, publishers went by names. If it is a book by a famous writer, they published it because they were sure of the sales. Even books by not so well-known writers were assured of a sale of a few thousand copies through public libraries, lending libraries, etc. But when the sales stopped, publishers withdrew from the scene. But a process of gradation, assessment, filtration, was never there in Telugu publishing at any time. It's a major flaw. There are no standard publishing procedures, and there is no guarantee that a book published by a particular publisher will be of quality.

What has been the response of readers and critics to your work? Are you satisfied with the critical scene in Telugu?

In 1987, my second novel *Swechcha* (*Freedom*) won the first prize in a competition. It got wide publicity and the magazine *Chatura* which had a good circulation published one lakh copies of the novel and they were all sold out. The magazine received a lot of letters about the novel from readers. For the first time I realized that a novel is read by so many people, that it can be read and understood in so many ways. It was an eye-opener. The editor of *Chatura*, Chalasani Prasad Rao, was a meticulous person. Unlike now, no contact number or address of the author used to be given in those days. So the magazine would get the letters, which were filed and given to the authors. The editor gave me three–four such files of readers' letters. From those letters, I could see that the common readers understood the novel well—understood it in the way I had intended—and appreciated it. At the same time, on the other hand, people with whom I worked—members of the Progressive Writers' Association, Revolutionary Writers' Association—were tearing the novel to pieces in their reviews and public discussions. It became clear to me then that these so-called critics could see only through their prejudiced eyes, and that their views are not what one should go by. My experience gave some clarity about criticism—that we don't have to bother about them, that what they want is different from what the common reader wants, and so we just have to write what we want to write. Readers' response is different and is often not partisan, and I seem to have been in sync with their thinking because my writing has always been well received by them. In general, I would say that constructive criticism is in extreme short supply in Telugu. For instance, very few critics take the trouble to do a detailed analysis of a book's components—its theme, style, imagery, characterization, etc.—as I did in *Athadu, aame, manam*. The lack of such criticism is a disadvantage for writers. It has come to such a pass that, today, if anyone attempts that kind of analysis, writers are unable to stomach it. They seem unwilling to take any comment that is not to their liking. By and large, it seems to me that the critics' hostility is the outcome not of incomprehension but of ideological prejudice.

But you have been an ideological writer yourself from the very beginning. So, does ideology limit a writer? Does it make the writer's response predictable?

I don't think there can be a writer without an ideological framework—whatever that ideology is—it is not possible. No one is neutral. But what is important is how the writer sees that ideology, understands it, and uses it in a systematic way to understand literature. In my case, for instance, I like the *Bharatam* very much—I read it, and know the poems by heart. I also adore the romantic poetry of Krishna Sastry[18], Nanduri's songs[19]. I am a Marxist, I know. While on the one hand I was working in the Students' Federation, on the other hand, I was writing love poems, like any other sixteen-year-old. For anyone with any poetic sense, it is impossible not to write love poetry, particularly at a certain age. But I never used to show it to my Student Federation friends for fear of being ridiculed for writing poetry about things like love. So such ideological constraints exist, I don't deny that. But many writers transcend those restrictions. It is important to observe how a writer views and understands human emotions. Love is a human emotion. So how beautifully and how tenderly a writer has presented that emotion is what one should look at instead of saying that you should not write love poetry at all because you're a Marxist. That is dogmatism, and I have never subscribed to such dogma. So,

I never faced that kind of ideological barriers while reading or writing. I don't think any of the great writers faced it either. Sri Sri, for instance, absorbed the entire literature and did not write simply by reading *Das Kapital.* He did not rewrite *Kapital* as *Mahaprasthanam* (1950). He could make those compounds fall into place because he had read *Kasi-khandam,*[20] and we as readers fell for them! So a writer transcends the ideological limits within the work. The critics don't seem to understand this at all! If you don't transcend such limitations, then you're not a creative writer.

How did the idea of Vimukta originate?

The stories in *Vimukta* were written at different times and were later put together. I first wrote 'Samaagamam' ('The Reunion') to counter Doordarshan's censorship, to show Surpanakha's suffering and how she overcame it. Once I wrote the story, I almost forgot about it. Then two years or so later, I wrote 'Mrunmaya naadam' ('The Music of the Earth'). I don't know how I wrote that story; I was in a trance. I never planned to write it or knew how I would do it. I only remember writing the first two–three lines. After that I don't know how it proceeded. I have never had such an experience. We all plan our stories, the starting point, development of the plot, characters, etc. Poetry can perhaps be written in a trance. But I don't know how I wrote that story. It must have come out from the depths of my unconscious. Something deep inside me must have been touched, I don't know what. Anyway, that made it two—stories of Surpanakha and Ahalya. Then I wanted to write a couple more around Sita. So I wrote about Urmila and Renuka consciously.

What is the intention in Vimukta*? Is the focus on Sita or the other women?*

Both. I wanted to show the kind of strength Sita got through others. It is not possible to achieve liberation all by ourselves, we need fellow groups—women or other exploited groups. Their experiences help us. Likewise, the experiences of these women help Sita. Sisterhood is an important concept in feminism. I have been able to grasp that concept through these stories. The other women are all Sita's sisters.

What has been the response to Vimukta?

It has received very good response. No negative responses at all! Even extreme traditionalists have responded quite positively and have appreciated its execution. I did not portray anyone as a villain, I described circumstances—historical and cultural contexts—in which women suffered and how they came out of them. I did not blame Rama or Ravana for Sita's plight. I took a balanced view which was well liked. Many readers told me that they felt that things must've happened exactly as I had narrated them. In fact, many people asked whether these stories are in the Ramayana itself. So, the stories have given me a lot of satisfaction.

Do you see this balanced approach as your evolved understanding of feminism?

Yes. Over a period of time one evolves a mature understanding and realizes that it is not a simple conflict between us and them, heroes and villains, but that there are larger issues which cannot be simply reduced to binaries.

Notes

1. Srirangam Srinivasarao (1910–1983)
2. Devarakonda Balagangadhara *Tilak* (1921–1966)

3. A group of six rebel poets who formed the group in 1965
4. Gudipati Venkata Chalam (1894–1979)
5. Kodavtiganti Kutumba Rao (1909–1980)
6. Panchadi Nirmala: a woman Naxalite leader from Srikakulam, killed in a police 'encounter' in 1969.
7. Rachakonda Viswanatha Sastry (1922–1993)
8. Pendyala Varavara Rao (1940–)
9. Baddam Bhaskara Reddy (1944–1982)
10. An analysis of Uppala Lakshmana Rao's novel of the same title published in 1950.
11. On 17 July 1985, in Karamchedu village of Prakasam district in Andhra Pradesh, several Dalits belonging to the Madiga caste were killed by upper caste landlords belonging to the Kamma caste.
12. Gurajada Venkata Apparao (1862–1915)
13. by Unnava Lakshminarayana (1877–1958)
14. The reference here is to Maxim Gorky's *Mother* (1906).
15. 'aasayaala kemo anantam, Appa Rao antati vaanni, andhratvam naa saapam' ('as for aims, they are infinite, I am an equal to Appa Rao, andhraness is my curse'; the reference here is to Gurajada Venkata Appa Rao, the author of *Kanyasulkam*); from the poem 'Aakhari maata modati maata' ('Last word first word') in *Khadga Srushti* (1966).
16. *Kanyasulkam*, a play by Gurajada Venkata Appa Rao, was first published in 1897. The revised and expanded version, which is now considered the standard edition, was published in 1909. The first complete translation in English was published in 2002.
17. *The Woman Unbound: Selected Short Stories* (1997)
18. Devulapalli Venkata Krishnasastri (1897–1980)
19. *Yenki Patalu* ('Songs of Yenki') by Nanduri Venkata Subbarao (1895–1957)
20. A kavya by the poet Srinatha

Translated from the Telugu by T. Vijay Kumar

HARPERPERENNIAL

Harper Perennial presents special editions of 10 of its finest books in translation

Bhima: Lone Warrior
M.T. Vasudevan Nair
Translated from the Malayalam by Gita Krishnankutty

Chemmeen
Thakazhi Sivasankara Pillai
Translated from the Malayalam by Anita Nair

Ghachar Ghochar
Vivek Shanbhag
Translated from the Kannada by Srinath Perur

Hindutva or Hind Swaraj
U.R. Ananthamurthy
Translated from the Kannada by Keerti Ramachandra & Vivek Shanbhag

The Liberation of Sita
Volga
Translated from the Telugu by T. Vijay Kumar & C. Vijayasree

A Life Misspent
Suryakant Tripathi Nirala
Translated from the Hindi by Satti Khanna

The Sea Lies Ahead
Intizar Husain
Translated from the Urdu by Rakhshanda Jalil

Selected Poems
Joy Goswami
Translated from the Bengali by Sampurna Chattarji

Wild Animals Prohibited: Stories/Anti-stories
Subimal Misra
Translated from the Bengali by V. Ramaswamy

Wild Words: Four Tamil Poets
Malathi Maithri, Salma, Kutti Revathi and Sukirtharani
Translated from the Tamil by Lakshmi Holmström